"What are you talking about, Button?"

Button.

Kat's heart squeezed.

The baby slapped the table and gave her dad a wide toothless smile. He planted a kiss on the side of her face, then went still, as if recalling that he and his daughter were not alone.

Oh yeah. Her heart had just officially melted, and she couldn't decide if it was because of the open affection Troy showed his daughter or the way his cheeks warmed when he'd realized she was watching.

"Have you thought about my proposition?" She kept her attention on the coffeepot as if it needed watching.

"Your cousin's behavior has nothing to do with you," Troy said, sounding as if he'd practiced the words. "You don't need to make it right."

Kat opened her mouth, but he stopped her by raising a finger. "I'm just putting that out there before I accept your offer."

It took Kat a moment to realize she didn't have a fight on

"Unless

Dear Reader,

Welcome to Larkspur, Montana, where you will meet the three spunky heroines of The Cowgirls of Larkspur Valley.

Kat Farley comes from a big ranch family that acts first and considers consequences second, and as a result chose to make herself a quiet life in a small city. But she missed home and when she gets the opportunity to head back to Larkspur, she takes it—and ends up with a cowboy as a tenant on her small farm.

Thrill-seeking rodeo rider Troy Mackay is a single dad who is looking to settle down and raise his daughter. He's determined to give his baby a stable, loving upbringing, and he can't be distracted by his attraction to Kat.

I've lived in the heart of ranch country for many years, and I love writing cowboys and cowgirls. I also love stories of growth and redemption, of characters facing their fears and coming out on top. Throw in some country charm, a few assorted animals and small-town characters, and you have what I like to write best.

I hope you enjoy *Home with the Rodeo Dad*. If you'd like to contact me or join my newsletter, check out my website, jeanniewatt.com. You can also find me on Facebook at Facebook.com/jeannie.watt.1.

Happy reading!

Jeannie

HEARTWARMING

Home with the Rodeo Dad

—

Jeannie Watt

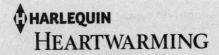

ISBN-13: 978-1-335-58482-3

Home with the Rodeo Dad

Copyright © 2023 by Jeannie Steinman

Recycling programs
for this product may
not exist in your area.

For questions and comments about the quality of this book,
please contact us at CustomerService@Harlequin.com.

Harlequin Enterprises ULC
22 Adelaide St. West, 41st Floor
Toronto, Ontario M5H 4E3, Canada
www.Harlequin.com

Printed in U.S.A.

Jeannie Watt lives on a small cattle ranch and hay farm in southwest Montana with her husband, her ridiculously energetic parents and the usual ranch menagerie. She spends her mornings writing, except during calving season, and during the remainder of the day enjoys sewing, doing glass mosaics and fixing fence. If you'd like more information about Jeannie and her books, please visit her website at jeanniewatt.com, where you can also sign up for her newsletter.

Books by Jeannie Watt

Harlequin Heartwarming

Sweet Home, Montana

Montana Homecoming
Montana Dad
A Ranch Between Them

Her Montana Cowboy

Harlequin Western Romance

Montana Bull Riders

The Bull Rider Meets His Match
The Bull Rider's Homecoming
A Bull Rider to Depend On
The Bull Rider's Plan

Visit the Author Profile page
at Harlequin.com for more titles.

I would like to dedicate this book to my beautiful daughter, Jamie Dallas, also a published author. I've had a blast pursuing our writing dreams together and it's wonderful to have someone in the family who "understands." I love you!

CHAPTER ONE

"Easy, Button. We're almost there."

Troy Mackay glanced in the rearview mirror of his Ford F-250 as his six-month-old daughter's warning cry became a full-fledged howl. His shoulders tightened in response, but he didn't panic like he would have only a few months ago.

Livia hit a particularly high note just as the headlights shone over a mailbox with a crooked flag, at which point he was supposed to turn left, according to the directions his new landlord had given him.

"Just another mile, kiddo."

Livia hiccupped, sucked in a breath and then howled again. Troy winced as he fought with himself to keep from stopping the truck right there.

An eternity later, which showed as four minutes on the dashboard clock, he rolled to a stop in front of a dark house and turned off the ignition. Livia went quiet, as if sensing that a big change was taking place.

It was.

Troy Mackay, former career rodeo rider was now Troy Mackay, single dad and full-time farrier. Or he would be full time as soon as he hung out his shingle and got Livia enrolled in the local daycare center.

Troy opened the rear door of the truck and unlatched the baby carrier. He was debating about whether to leave Livia strapped in or take her out and hold her when the porch light came on behind him.

He whirled toward the light, wondering if a place this old had motion sensors, then he saw movement in the reflected light on the windows. There was someone in the house. Quickly, he relatched the baby carrier, closed the door and stood protectively in front of the truck. This house was supposed to be empty, so what was he facing?

A squatter taking refuge, maybe?

Livia let out a howl that shattered the stillness of the night.

Get in the truck and drive. Come back in the morning.

The need to protect his daughter was paramount, and Troy was about to do just that, even though he had no place to go. Then the front door opened, and a young woman stepped out, hugging her long sweater around her body.

"Hi," he called in the friendliest voice he could manage. "Maybe I'm at the wrong place. I'm looking for Littlegate Farm."

"Why?" The woman pulled her sweater more tightly around her, and her chin lifted as she spoke.

Troy shifted his weight, perplexed by the woman's tone. "Because I rented it."

Her back stiffened. "I don't think so."

He frowned. "I have a contract."

"No."

"You want to see it?" he asked.

"No need. It's not valid."

Troy cocked his head stubbornly. "How so?"

"I own Littlegate Farm, and I promise you that I haven't rented it to anyone."

IF IT WASN'T for the baby crying in the pickup truck, Kat Farley would have called the sheriff and told him there was a guy standing on her driveway pretending that he had a right to be on her property. She still might do that, but first she was going to get more information, like who was this guy, and why did he think he'd rented this place?

Was he scamming her? There was no law saying scam artists couldn't have babies.

Kat took an unconscious backward step. She might have taken another if the guy hadn't kicked the dirt in front of him in frustration. He planted his hands on his hips and looked back at the truck as if he had no idea what his next move might be. Was he a great actor? Was this part of a bigger plan on his part? After recent events, she no longer trusted her judgment when it came to sussing out people's true agendas.

"I don't understand," he finally said in a voice that did not smack of subterfuge. "I signed a contract to rent a place called Littlegate Farm for six months. This—" he pointed at the ground in front of him "—is Littlegate Farm?"

"There's only one." Kat wrapped her cardigan more tightly around her midsection as she took a cautious step forward to better see the guy, who stood just inside the pool of light cast by the bulb over her head. He was of average height, whipcord lean, but his shoulders indicated he was no stranger to physical labor. She couldn't see his face beneath the felt cowboy hat, but she had a sense of angles.

"Who are you?"

"My name is Troy Mackay." He jerked his head toward the truck. "My daughter, Livia."

"Who rented the property to you?"

Her heart started beating a little faster as she waited for the reply that would hopefully clear up this mess.

"A work acquaintance of mine. Arlie Stokes."

Kat stared at him for a frozen moment, then she tipped her head back with an exasperated exhalation. Arlie was the opportunist of the family, and it appeared that he'd come up with a way to earn some side cash.

"You know him?" There was a note of hope in Troy Mackay's voice.

"He's my cousin. His mom sold me this place. It isn't his to rent."

The sale had gone through so rapidly that Arlie could have been unaware, but he still had no right to rent his mother's property.

"Then…"

She didn't answer because she had no answer other than to send this guy on his way. This wasn't a situation of her making, and she'd promised herself upon moving home that she wouldn't get sucked into family drama, even as a small voice had whispered, "Fat chance."

Score one for the small voice.

"I don't have Arlie's number," she said.

"I do." He pulled out his phone and searched his contacts, then he held the phone to his ear. The seconds ticked by, and his expression grew grimmer. Lowering the phone, he shook his head as the baby gave a heartrending cry from the interior of the truck.

Troy turned on his heel, strode to the

truck and reached inside to fiddle with some straps. A moment later, he gently eased out a baby wearing a fuzzy sleeper and trailing a blanket, which dropped to the ground. He expertly balanced the baby against his hip and bent to pick it up.

Okay. This was his baby, not a prop in a scam.

He lifted the little girl to rest against his shoulder, murmuring to her while Kat watched. She wondered if he was taking advantage of the moment to garner sympathy or if he was a concerned dad comforting his baby.

The baby eventually quieted, but Troy kept rubbing her back through the fuzzy sleeper as he turned to Kat.

"I don't know what to do," he said.

She had the feeling that if it had just been him, he would have driven away and hunted down Arlie, but with the baby, he was honestly searching for answers.

"There's some decent motels in town."

"That's an option," he agreed.

"But..."

"But your cousin pretty much emptied

me of cash." He stared past her in the general direction of the house as he confessed, "I've had a run on my finances lately. I don't want to drop a hundred bucks on a room for ten hours if I don't have to." He glanced back at her. "Do you have any idea how much diapers cost?"

Kat slowly shook her head, hating the corner she felt herself being backed into. She was not going to open her home to a stranger. Not even one with a baby.

A thought struck her.

"You can stay at my parents' ranch on the other side of the valley."

"I don't think—"

"Trust me. They embrace this kind of stuff." But Kat could understand his hesitation, and she didn't want to send him on the twenty-mile drive across the valley with a tired, crying baby. Town was closer. "I'll loan you the money for the motel room. We can meet tomorrow to talk about this."

"Thanks, but no." Troy turned and headed back to the truck. He opened the front and rear doors, and once again settled his daughter in the carrier.

"Where did you work with Arlie?"

He turned to look at her. "Michaels Short Haul Trucking. Kalispell."

That sounded right. Arlie had been in Kalispell the last she'd heard, and he did contract trucking.

"The owners sold out and retired," Troy added. "Arlie offered me this place before we parted ways."

"When was that?"

"Last week. Arlie said something about going on vacation before looking for his next contract, which might be why I can't raise him."

Kat could see that Troy believed that theory about as much as she did. Arlie was probably lying low.

"All right." The words left Kat's lips before she could stop them. Troy frowned, and so did she. "You can stay here for one night, but I don't have any beds." She folded her arms over her midsection. "Yet. I'm in the process of moving in."

He studied her from where he stood next to the truck, apparently weighing options, making her realize that he might be as cautious about this as she was. After all, he had a baby to look out for.

"The bedrooms have locks." The old-fashioned kind with keys, and the solid wood doors were sturdy.

Troy hesitated and then pulled Livia back out of the carrier and settled her against him. "I hate to impose, but... I'm in a spot here."

A spot her cousin had put him in. How was she supposed to send him on his way in the middle of the night?

"It's the sensible thing to do," she said. "It's late, and your baby needs to get in out of the cold."

Once again Troy hesitated as if desperately searching for an option that didn't involve her or her family or dropping some of the little cash he had left. Apparently, he came up empty, because he reached inside the truck and pulled out a folding contraption that had to be a baby bed, then he and his daughter headed up the walk to the house that he'd thought would be his for the next few months.

When Kat saw her elusive cousin again,

she was going to do him some harm. In the meantime, she'd call her family, apprise them of the situation in a voice loud enough to let Troy know that she had backup if necessary.

Several minutes later, after Troy had set up the baby bed and she'd found a pan in one of her still-unpacked kitchen boxes for him to use to warm baby formula in, she interrupted her mother's late-evening oil-painting session and explained the events that had just unfolded on Littlegate Farm.

"Put him on the line," Emily Farley said.

"What? No, Mom. I can handle this." She lowered her voice to hiss into the phone. "I understand your concern, but I have this under control." She raised her voice to a normal level and glanced toward the kitchen as she said, "I just wanted to tell you what was going on and to ask if anyone had heard from Arlie lately."

"I haven't, but I'll check with your brothers. Andrew's close to Kalispell. He might know something. And Kent always seems to know stuff no one else does."

"Thanks, Mom. I'll keep you posted."

She cleared her throat and then added in an undertone, "Don't worry."

"If you say you have this under control, I believe you."

She had good reason. Kat was the Farley child who thought things through and considered consequences before acting. The one who'd built a safe and predictable life crunching numbers and putting money into a retirement fund. Not that she was a wimp. No one who'd grown up on the Farley Ranch could be considered that, but Kat was the only one in her family who felt the urge to freak out over situations that, well, required a freak-out.

Her mother was blessed with a personality that allowed her to face with equanimity the various inappropriate creatures her sons regularly brought into the house, the occasional fire or minor explosion, and the random broken bones.

The ranch stumbled along with no real plan of action other than a certainty that everything would turn out all right in the end. The ridiculous thing was that, so far, it had. Farley luck, her dad called it. He believed in it, as did her brothers. That belief was as much a part of her brothers' personalities as was their need to push that envelope just a *little* further than sanity deemed safe.

Kat did not believe in Farley luck, nor did she have the unwavering belief that everything would work out in the end. Kat's recent experience with Derek Cashman spoke to that. Although, upon reflection, she had to admit that things *had* worked out in a grim sort of way. Discovering the truth about the man she'd hoped to marry had the unexpected effect of kicking a long-dormant Farley gene to life. Instead of retreating and considering options, Kat had done the opposite. She'd made a move.

A Farley-esque move.

An in-your-face-Derek move.

She'd bought Littlegate Farm, and she'd done it without properly vetting the situation—something she never ever did. She'd managed to squish the doubts and misgivings that had arisen in the days following her rash decision instead of mulling them over to see if they were valid. Of course they were.

She'd impulse-bought a farm to teach a lesson to the guy who'd lied to her and manipulated her. A guy who'd told his brother that he'd have no trouble bringing her around to his way of thinking because she always gave in to him eventually. That was one thing he liked about her. She was compliant.

Kat's jaw muscles tightened at the memory, and she forced herself to relax, to take a long deep breath and let it out slowly. It was a technique she'd learned during childhood.

She'd thought she and Derek were building a life together, but he'd celebrated the fact that he could manipulate her into doing what he wanted. The kicker was that she *had* given in to Derek's wishes too often in a misguided effort to be a good partner, rarely rocking the boat when differences arose. Now she knew he'd taken advantage of her and candidly discussed it with his brother. She felt stupid and angry and utterly determined to never let anything like that happen again.

She hadn't a clue Derek was playing her until her Aunt Margo offered her first refusal on Littlegate Farm before it went on the market. Buying had seemed like a no-brainer, but Derek had immediately tried to dissuade her. At the time, she'd been perplexed. She had the funds to make the down payment and plans to lease the place, thus making it self-supporting.

After overhearing Derek's phone call to his brother, Dane, she'd pieced things together. Dane was a real estate hotshot in Larkspur, and he wanted the property. Kat didn't know if he wanted it for himself or to sell for the commission, but it didn't matter. She loved Littlegate Farm, and she wasn't going to let it slip away from her.

Her first instinct after overhearing the conversation was to walk into the room where her supposed beau was plotting on the phone with his brother and have it out with him. Instead, she'd let herself out of the house as quietly as she'd come in and set about buying Littlegate Farm.

For two days, Derek had worked on her, and for two days, she'd silently seethed over his duplicity and her poor judgment. She'd waited for the money to transfer and her aunt to countersign the agreement, and the way Derek placated, charmed and gently coerced had taken on a whole new look. He was a master of making her think his concern was centered on her when he only cared about himself.

Why hadn't she seen this earlier?

Because she was used to honest people who said what they meant? Or because she lacked insight? The evidence was before her. She'd totally misread Derek. It didn't help that even though they'd never said anything, she sensed that her best friends, Whitney Fox and Maddie Kincaid, had never fully embraced Derek. She'd told herself they didn't know him, but she'd come to find out that was her issue.

In the end, after she'd told him she'd purchased the farm, she'd had the satisfaction of telling him they were done. He'd shown no regret and told her she had no idea what she was getting into. That she would regret her headstrong behavior. That things could happen that she wasn't in a position to handle.

Kat went still at the thought and then

craned her neck to study Troy standing at the stove with his daughter on his shoulder. Could it be?

No.

Not Derek's style. Definitely more of an Arlie move, and Kat had a feeling that after the sting wore off, the Cashman brothers wouldn't bother her. She hoped so anyway. Derek wasn't used to being shut down or found out, and she'd done just that. Would he engage in petty revenge?

If he does, you'll deal with it. Right now, you have a situation.

As if on cue, Troy stepped into the living room, cradling his daughter in one arm as he fed her. She patted the bottle as she drank. He smiled down at her and then indicated the packing boxes along one wall of the living room with a lift of his chin. "You haven't been here long."

"Nope. Our positions could have easily been reversed." She could only imagine how she would have reacted if she'd found Troy and his baby in residence when she'd arrived.

A rustling sounded overhead, and they both glanced up, Troy frowning.

"I have an uninvited roommate," Kat said. The house had lain empty for the better part of a year, allowing the local critters to take advantage. Thankfully, the mice hadn't yet found their way in through the many caulked cracks, but the attic was another matter.

"Appears that way." Troy slowly paced as his daughter ate. "I guess," he said slowly, resignedly, "if something appears to be too perfect, it's wise to consider the possibility that it might be."

"Do you have a job here?"

"I will." He kept his eyes on his daughter, who stared back at him over the bottle. "My previous job, the one where I met Arlie, came to an unexpected end. The owners got a buyout offer and took it. Thanks to their recommendation, I got a job here with L&S Sand and Gravel, but it doesn't start until September, when one of their drivers retires."

"And Arlie offered this place?"

"Like I said. Perfect. I was going to spend

the summer shoeing horses, then go to work full time for the gravel operation after Labor Day."

"You're a farrier?"

"I am. Farrier, truck driver."

He sounded a lot like her brothers and their friends—guys who worked with their hands and took pride in what they did.

"You?" he asked politely before readjusting the bottle so that Livia could get the last little bit.

"Paper pusher."

Nothing to be ashamed of, but her secure, safe job with excellent benefits and a 401(k) was not exactly colorful…and it was a touch boring. Maybe too boring in and of itself. She'd suspected for some time that she'd made a mistake in her career choice; that all of her planning and careful reasoning, done in the name of being the responsible Farley child, had led her down the wrong path.

She'd told herself it was normal to feel restless, and that all she needed was a hobby. But hobbies didn't help, and the feeling of restlessness grew, making her suspect that she was more like her wild brothers than she'd once believed. Maybe the occasional explosion was a good thing.

Kat's phone rang, making her jump. She checked the screen and then stifled a groan. "My brother," she said before answering.

Troy took the hint and carried the baby into the kitchen.

"Mom called. I'll be right over," James said without bothering with a hello. Loud country music played in the background, telling Kat that her brother probably wasn't at home.

"No, you will not." It was close to eleven. "I'm fine. He just fed his baby, and all is well."

"Did Mom get the name right? Troy Mackay?"

"Yes."

"Medium-size guy, dark hair?"

"Do you know him?"

"He's areally decent bronc rider. Or he was. He's pretty popular with the ladies."

"Right now, I think he's only concerned about one lady. His little girl, who's about to be put down for the night."

Did kids her age sleep through the night?

She'd undoubtedly find out in short order. The last thing Kat needed was for James to wake everyone up if they did manage to go to sleep.

"Thanks for the offer. You can stop by for breakfast."

From the kitchen, she heard Troy emptying the pan of water into the sink.

"I think—"

"Please do not come by and wake up this baby," Kat said. "None of us will thank you. Mom and Dad know the situation, and so do you. My bases are covered."

For being people who laughed at fate, her family seemed ridiculously protective of her, as if she couldn't handle anything out of the norm.

Well, she could. She had a vagabond cowboy and a baby in her kitchen, and she was handling the situation just fine, thank you very much.

LIVIA SIGHED IN her sleep, shifted positions and then settled again, and Troy's taut muscles relaxed an iota.

Having a child changes everything.

Tiff had said that before their marriage had gone rocky, which had been almost immediately, calling him baby crazy for simply having suggested that they start a family after he retired from rodeo. When the sad truth about their union became apparent, he'd dropped the idea, and within a year, he knew that his impulsive marriage was not going to last. He'd loved Tiff, and Tiff loved herself, and that was that.

When she'd discovered she was pregnant after their divorce, she'd told him. She'd carried Livia to term with the understanding that for all intents and purposes, she was a surrogate. Tiff did not have a maternal bone in her body. She'd given birth to a beautiful baby girl and handed her over to a terrified Troy before heading across the country to start what she called her new life. He hadn't heard a word from her since, nor did he expect to.

It was him and Livia against the world. And the world had just taken a swing at them. *Thank you, Arlie Stokes.* Troy fought back a surge of anger. Hating on Arlie wasn't going to get him anywhere.

Tough. He was going to hate on the guy anyway. Anger felt good. Cathartic.

Justified.

He pulled in a deep breath, frowning through the darkness at the rustling sounds overhead. Too big for mice. Possibly a raccoon. He took hold of the leg of the bassinet and pulled it closer to his bedroll.

Tomorrow, he would hunt down Arlie and demand his money back. Somehow. Montana was a big state, and Arlie had a truck he contracted out. Who knew if he was even still in the state?

Troy scowled at the ceiling. The odds of finding Arlie were slim. The chance of getting more than a promise to pay Troy back were probably even slimmer. Troy had witnessed firsthand Arlie's lack of care with his finances. If a shiny truck accessory caught his eye, the man bought it. Round of drinks? On him.

Getting his money back was going to be a process, and he didn't have enough of the stuff to search for the man who'd cheated him.

He muttered a curse at the ceiling.

If it wasn't for Livia, he'd be after Arlie in a heartbeat. Until his daughter had come into his life, he'd had no qualms about stepping into the unknown.

Those days were gone for the next eighteen years. He was a dad, and he had a daughter to care for, which meant that he needed to find a place to live and a job—any job—plus a sitter he trusted while he worked at that job, all in a community where he knew no one, except for the woman who'd taken pity on him.

A woman related to the man who'd cheated him.

Troy brushed the thought aside. Should he call his dad? His stomach knotted at the idea. Not only would he have to crawl on his belly, but odds were good that his dad would also take delight in hitting the Deny button, as he had when Troy had made a stab at amends five years after the fight that had ended their relationship.

That had stung, and Troy's pride wasn't up for taking another hit.

He would try again if things got too hairy, for Livia's sake—and it would only be for her sake. Maybe the parent gene and the grandparent gene were not connected... except that when he'd texted his dad the news of Livia's birth, all he'd gotten back was a terse "Congratulations" and not one word since.

His parents were no more interested in grandparenting than they'd been in parenting.

He rolled over onto his side, wincing a little. Years of bronc riding had made it tougher to sleep on a hard floor than in the past, and he needed to sleep. If Livia made it through the night, she'd be up early, hungry and wet. And he needed to have a clear head if he was going to figure a way out of this mess.

His mind strayed to the woman who'd been unwittingly involved in her cousin's scheme. Kat. He hadn't caught her last name because his brain had been busy scrambling for a solution to his immediate problem. But he had noted the somewhat wild state of her long curly brown hair and the direct way her aqua eyes met his.

Aqua.

Not a word he normally used, but it was the word for those eyes.

He tucked a hand under his head, shifting mental focus. What was his next move?

A part of him longed for the days when not knowing his next move wouldn't have interfered with his sleep or his peace of mind. The days when he'd had faith that he'd come up with something.

But now he had a little girl, and he owed her—and himself, really—a secure life. He'd promised her that the first time he'd held her and stared down into her amazing little face.

Six months in, and he was going down in flames.

CHAPTER TWO

HOLY SMOKE.

Kat should be sleeping, or trying to, but the Google search for Troy Mackay had proven interesting beyond imagination.

Okay, that was pushing it, because thanks to her upbringing and the hair-raising stunts her brothers pulled, she had a very wild imagination.

She'd found out Troy Mackay was more than a farrier and truck driver. He was a rich boy who'd indulged in all kinds of extreme sports as a teen. He'd been featured in an article about thrill seekers, and there'd been photos of him smiling in the face of danger. That smile had been broad and carefree, his expression clearly stating he could handle anything. Whatever *anything* might be.

It appeared from her online research that there were a lot of anythings. Skydiving, base jumping, motocross, extreme skiing, free climbing and finally rodeo, where he seemed to have concentrated his efforts during his twenties. From what she could tell, he'd had a respectable career and made the National Finals three times. Then he'd dropped off the radar midseason last year due to an injury.

Now he was in her spare bedroom.

Kat set her phone aside and glanced up at the ceiling. The overhead resident had finally quieted. Her mind had not.

She'd read the desperation in the guy's face when he'd realized the truth of the situation. There'd been a brief moment of defeat, followed by a wave of determination. He had a kid to take care of.

Troy Mackay was obviously a proud man, and the only reason he was here now, instead of sleeping in his truck somewhere, was because of his daughter.

She wasn't responsible for Arlie's actions, and she wouldn't break her promise to herself not to take on family drama, but she wanted to help this guy out of this mess—for his baby's sake, if nothing else. The question was how?

TROY RECOGNIZED JAMES FARLEY as soon as the man walked through the farmhouse door. James was a talented steer wrestler, being big, aggressive and agile, but as far as Troy knew, the man never competed outside of Montana.

Troy, on the other hand, had made rodeo his life after being cut off by his appearance-sensitive parents. Like his ex-wife, Myra and Daniel Mackay should never have had children. Unfortunately, they didn't come to this conclusion until after Troy was born.

Granted, he'd lacked for nothing during his childhood, except for parental attention. Part of him had relished his freedom—freedom his peers hadn't enjoyed—but another part had longed for the closeness of family. He'd done his best to garner attention, with his efforts escalating as he grew older. Extreme sports, skydiving, free climbing—anything with a decent edge of danger… Nothing had seemed to bother his parents until he'd discovered rodeo at the age of seventeen. That didn't fit the Mackay social image the way the other, more costly sports had. It was one thing having a daredevil son who threw himself out of airplanes and another to have one with horse manure on his boots. Maybe that was why rodeo had become the center of his world. Negative attention was better than none at all.

The weird thing was that his parents still expected him to do the son thing—to go to college, major in business, join the family firm. Keep up appearances. The Mackays would continue to look like a family, but they wouldn't be a family. Troy had refused, and he'd been cut off. Financially. Physically. He'd also say emotionally, but there hadn't been a lot of emotions displayed over the years. He suspected that his parents had feelings toward him, but they were of the old-school mindset, where kids toed the line or got cut off.

Frankly, he had no idea what went on in his parents' heads, but he knew that they had a firm idea of how things were supposed to be and did not deviate from it.

After Troy's split with his parents, there'd been a steep learning curve as he negotiated life without limitless resources. He became rather good at it, and as time passed and his rodeo career flourished, he took pride in his ability to fend for himself.

He'd trained to shoe horses and got a CDL so that he could haul stock for a Red Angus outfit during the off-season. He got his hands dirty every day that he wasn't on the rodeo circuit, and he loved it. His parents did not reach out to him after his disastrous attempt to make good with them. That was the reality of his relationship with them. They would never be Mom and Dad.

Things would be different for his kid. She might not have tons of money, but she'd have a father, and she'd have love—although he wouldn't have minded having both money and love to give.

"James Farley," the big man said, extending his hand. "Kat's brother."

"I remember you." Troy adjusted Livia in the crook of his arm as he reached his free hand across the table—the only furniture in the entire house—to shake James's hand. "Good to see you."

James's handshake was firm, with just a small warning squeeze at the end, but he smiled, first at Troy, then at Livia.

"Kat tells me there's an issue with Arlie."

James went to the stove as he spoke and poured a cup of coffee from the old-fashioned percolator. After dumping several spoons of sugar straight out of the bag into the cup, he settled himself on the chair opposite Troy. He began stirring the coffee when Kat came into the room.

"You said no to breakfast," she reminded him.

"I got hungry." He took the spoon out of the coffee and set it on the bare wood of the unfinished table. "And I wanted to drop by."

Troy couldn't say that he blamed the guy. If he had a sister—or if this was something his rodeo travel partner, Saskia Belmont, had gotten herself into—he'd have concerns. He wouldn't want a strange guy spending the night under her roof, not even if he'd been as exhausted as Troy had been the previous evening.

He'd slept like the dead, and fortunately, Livia had lasted until six in the morning, giving him an uninterrupted night for once. But now that morning had come, he had to figure out his next move.

"Have you been home?" Kat glanced toward the window. "Or did you sleep in your truck in my front yard?"

"I went home," James said, lifting his cup to his lips. "It's not a repeat of the Derek thing."

Troy was intrigued by Kat's assumption that her brother would sleep in his truck in her front yard and by what the *Derek thing* might be. James shifted his attention from his sister to Livia.

"Cute kid."

"I think so."

"Where's her mom?"

"James!" Kat nearly choked.

"Not in the picture," Troy said in a way that made it clear the whereabouts of Livia's mother was no one's business. Then he decided that he had to come clean, because why not? "Livia's mom relinquished custody. I'm her sole parent."

The silence following his explanation was palpable. Kat cleared her throat and pointedly changed the subject. "I think we need to consider what to do about Arlie cheating Troy."

"I asked around last night after you called, and no one has seen him lately." James shifted his attention to Troy. "Where did you guys hammer out this deal?"

"We were working for Michael's Short Haul out of Kalispell. When the company was sold, I got a job with L&S Sand and Gravel here in Larkspur, but it doesn't start until fall. I told Arlie I was going to move early since it's so expensive living near Glacier. He offered me this place, and we did a handshake on a six-month lease." Troy gave a little shrug. "I planned to shoe horses to make ends meet until the job starts, and he assured me that Larkspur could use more farriers."

"That's true," James said. "If you're any good, that is."

Kat pressed her lips together as if choosing her battles. Her brother, it appeared, had no filter.

"I'm good," Troy said simply. He'd apprenticed with one of the best farriers in the state while off from rodeo and kept in practice during the season.

"And you said Arlie said something about taking a vacation?" Kat asked.

"He left a couple days before me." Tony adjusted Livia's position on his arm. It was getting numb, but since she was now sound asleep, he wasn't about to put her down and risk waking her. "He talks a good game," Troy said. "Showed me pictures of the place and everything."

It had seemed like a dream come true. Now it was more like a nightmare.

"How were you supposed to get the rent to Arlie?" James asked. "And for that matter, how much did you pay up front?"

"First, last and damage deposit. In cash. And after that, I was supposed to send money orders to a post office box in Kalispell."

"We'll make this right," Kat said, taking a seat at the table between the two men.

"Somehow," she added on a less optimistic note.

"I'll put 'Hunt Arlie down' at the top of my to-do list," James said before gesturing at his sister with the coffee cup. "I think he's been renting out Littlegate Farm since Aunt Margo broke her hip and went into the assisted care facility. One of the guys at the pub knew someone who lived here in January."

"Figures," Kat said. "And you can bet he was not sharing the rental money with his mother."

"I wonder if he knew that she sold the place to you."

"I'd give it even odds," Kat said. She put her palms on the table in front of her. "I'm not telling Aunt Margo about this, and neither are you. She has enough to deal with without finding out that her son has been up to his usual crap."

There was a brief silence as the brother and sister studied the table in front of them, then James lifted his chin.

"Okay. Here's what we're going to do."

Troy noted the almost comical look of

alarm that crossed Kat's face at his pronouncement. Before James could continue, Kat held up a hand, and Troy was surprised to see the big man instantly close his mouth.

"Yes. You'll go back to the ranch and bring the camp trailer here. Andrew doesn't need it anymore, right?" She waited for James's nod before meeting Troy's gaze. "You and Livia can stay in it until you come up with a plan B. And maybe we can hunt down Arlie and get your money back."

"I don't..." Troy closed his mouth. His first instinct was to say no, but the baby who slept heavily in his arms made him think twice. He was no longer in a position to head off into the unknown, assuming he'd figure things out before disaster struck.

Kat reached out and touched the back of his hand, startling him. "Consider this payback for what our cousin did to you." She didn't mention Livia, but her gaze rested for a moment on his sleeping daughter. "We'll settle up after this gets sorted out." He had a feeling that there was more she wanted to say but wasn't going to, perhaps because her brother was here.

Troy glanced from Kat to James and gave a nod of approval to his sister's plan.

Livia stirred then, pushed back against his shoulder and looked at him with sleepy blue eyes before her mouth turned down, and she started to cry. Why? He had no idea. It could be a diaper, it could be a stomachache, it could be nothing, but he was immediately in full parent mode.

He pushed his chair back and got to his feet, jiggling the baby as he stood looking down at Kat and James. "Thank you," he said.

They could work out details later, but for now, he had a roof over his and Livia's heads, and that was more than he'd hoped for before he'd finally fallen into an exhausted sleep the night before.

"Not a problem," James said with a wave of his big hand.

Kat simply nodded as she studied him with those amazing bluish-green eyes. He nodded back and then turned his attention to Livia. "If you'll excuse us, I have a diaper to attend to."

"Better you than me," James said with a laugh and pushed himself to his feet. "I'll be back early afternoon, say one-ish."

"Great," Kat said as Troy carried his daughter out of the room.

Yes. Great. He totally appreciated this... and totally hated being in a position where he had to take this kind of help.

Got a situation here...

KAT HIT SEND, and the text whooshed off into the ether around lunchtime. She hadn't immediately alerted her friends about the odd situation she found herself in because she'd needed a little time to work through the harm that Arlie had done. Ultimately, she'd decided that she needed a sounding board. Someone other than James.

She and her two best friends since middle school, Maddie Kincaid and Whitney Fox, had formed a message group years ago to keep up with one another's busy lives in the moment rather than waiting for a good time to call. "Got a situation here" was the code phrase they'd used since high school to indicate that something funny, earth-shattering or strange had occurred in their lives.

They didn't see each other as often as they once did, due to distances and jobs, but they stayed in touch and met whenever they could. Now that she'd moved from Spokane to Larkspur and was living closer to her friends, she hoped for more face time. The real kind.

What?

Maddie's response was almost instantaneous. Her friend was busy juggling a demanding job as the co-owner of a wedding boutique along with preparations for her own wedding in December, but she apparently had a moment of downtime.

Whitney's response quickly zinged in after Maddie's.

Is there a problem with the farm?

My cousin rented it to a stranger. The guy is now here with his baby.

WHAT? Maddie demanded.

A string of questioning emojis from Whitney followed, and Kat tapped out a brief explanation of what her cousin had done.

Your cousin bites.

Kat wholeheartedly agreed with Whitney.
Troy Mackay as in rodeo Troy Mackay? Maddie asked.

He rodeoed.

Kat wasn't surprised that Maddie had heard of the guy. Maddie was a barrel racer, and she followed all things cowboy.

How old is the baby?

Dunno. She replied to Whit. Maybe five or six months?
I'll be in town day after tomorrow, Whitney wrote. Let's meet. You available, Mad?

Dress fitting for a client. A sad emoji followed. But maybe...

The rumble of the trailer arriving brought Kat's head up.

Gotta go. Keep this quiet for now, okay?

She received two thumbs-up emojis in rapid succession, put the phone down and went to the door.

James's truck rolled to a stop as Kat stepped out onto the porch. Troy had decided to go along to help, taking his little daughter with him even though Kat had offered to babysit. Troy had politely turned her down, but it had been very clear that until he knew her better, there would be no babysitting.

Kat pushed her hair from her forehead with the back of her hand and started down the steps. The trailer was in better shape than she remembered, but she was certain it needed a good cleaning. Did she offer to help with that? She had her own house-cleaning to do, but he had a baby.

Play it by ear.

She had kind of a theme developing here.

"We went through the trailer," James said as Kat approached. "Everything looks good. Andrew tidied it up to impress a woman a few months back, and since hunting season is not yet upon us, he hasn't had opportunity to untidy it."

Kat opened the door and took a sniff. The interior smelled of air freshener, and Andrew had done a decent job of cleaning up. There was a layer of dust, but that was to be expected. The usual jumble of clothing and sports equipment from either a trip to the lake or to the mountains was gone.

"I really appreciate this," Troy said from where he stood at the front of the truck. She could tell he was trying to sound positive but wasn't feeling it, and Kat couldn't blame him. Losing all that money had to be eating at him, and relying on them to put a roof over his kid's head… She totally got it. But she did wonder why he was in this financial pickle to begin with since he came from wealthy parents?

None of her business.

"Not a problem," she said. "I'm just glad that the trailer is in good shape."

"Our brother is kind of a slob at times," James added. "We can hook up to electricity there." He pointed at the barn.

"That'd be great," Troy said in the same polite voice.

Kat gestured at the baby sleeping in the carrier seat. "If you want, we could take her to the porch, and I'll keep an eye on her while you guys set things up?"

"Sure." Troy unfastened the carrier and then headed up the walk to set his sleeping daughter in the shade next to the wicker chair. "If she cries, give a yell." He smiled a little. "Actually, I'll probably hear her."

"Probably," Kat agreed, and their gazes connected just long enough for her to feel a micro jolt of...what? She didn't know, but whatever it was had bumped up her heart rate.

Troy headed down the walk to the trailer that James was now expertly situating next to the barn. He slid it between the rustic building and the cottonwood tree that would provide decent shade during the heat of the day. Kat settled in the wicker chair next to the sleeping baby. She glanced down at the little girl, marveling at the length of her lashes and the perfect bow of her mouth.

"You have a good dad," she murmured before shifting her attention back to the trailer and Troy, who was now giving James hand signals as her brother backed up.

A good, overly proud, ridiculously good-looking dad who appeared to have some issues in the trust department.

Of course, none of that was really any concern of hers.

AFTER THE CAMP trailer was leveled and connected to power, James gave his sister a hug that lifted her off her feet, saluted Troy, got into his truck and drove away. Kat and Troy stood a few feet from his temporary home, Livia happily plucking at the fabric of his shirt with her little fingers.

He was overwhelmed by the events of the last eighteen hours and dealing with a case of simmering anger that he would explore once he was alone. In less than a day, he'd discovered that he'd been swindled out of a healthy amount of cash, had no place to live and was now dependent on the kindness of strangers while he sorted things out.

None of that sat well. As he'd told Kat, he wasn't a receive-charity kind of guy. After being cut off by his parents, it had taken him a while to get used to not having everything he wanted—or for a time, anything he wanted—but once he achieved autonomy, there'd been no looking back. In fact, he was a little ashamed of all he'd taken for granted while living on his parents' dime.

Livia let out a happy crow as she patted his shirt, and Kat smiled at the baby before glancing at Troy.

"Would you like help cleaning?"

More things to be beholden for? He thought not.

He pointed toward her house with his chin. "I think you have enough on your plate without adding me to the list."

"I don't have a baby," she said as Livia buried her face against his shoulder.

"I've learned to function pretty well with her."

Kat bit her lip. She looked like she wanted to say more but seemed to think better of it. "You're right. I've got a bit to do." She smiled at Livia and then turned to go, wrapping her oversized flannel shirt around herself as she moved.

"Hey."

She stopped and glanced back.

"I don't mean to sound ungrateful." But he knew he'd come off that way. "I appreciate you guys hauling this trailer over here and letting me stay while I figure a few things out." He shifted his weight. "More than you know."

Kat shrugged in reply.

"I'll be here for the shortest time possible."

Kat canted her head to one side as the wind lifted the curls from her shoulders, creating a halo effect around her head. "No hurry." She smoothed her hair after the gust had passed. "You're welcome to stay."

He wasn't aware of a shift in his expression, but Kat must have picked up on something, because she added, "We're not only doing this because of Arlie cheating you."

"Why else would you?" The question fell from his lips before he could stop it. "What I mean—"

"You think I have an ulterior motive?" She gave him a perplexed look. "Might I ask what on earth you think that would be?"

Point taken.

He closed his mouth before he got himself in deeper. It was obvious she was also doing this because of Livia, who was now babbling as she pulled at his collar. He could deal with that. Sometimes a guy had to put aside his pride and live with a little discomfort for the sake of others. Like the most important person in his world. He rubbed his daughter's back, turning his head to pull in the sweet scent of her hair before shifting her in his arms.

"Little secret, Troy." Her lips curved

softly. "No one likes being in a position where they're beholden to others. But it happens."

"How would you feel if it happened to you?"

"Rotten, but I'd try to remind myself that I could pay it back to the universe in the future." With a lift of her eyebrows, she turned and headed toward her house.

THE RICH SCENT of brownies filled the kitchen. It had taken some effort to go through her half-unpacked kitchen boxes to find the mix and the correct size pan, but the result was worth it. Kat felt better just smelling them.

She wasn't responsible for what Arlie had done, but she felt bad about it. After a little digging, she'd discovered that he had indeed been renting the house out regularly since his mother had gone into care after breaking her hip. It was a nice little side gig, and Kat took comfort in the fact that he hadn't heartlessly targeted a man with a baby. He probably wasn't aware that the sale had gone through.

But it had, and now she had a tenant. A hesitant tenant, but honestly, she wouldn't mind if he stayed. There were pluses to having a warm body on the property. Without him here, she'd be alone, miles from the nearest neighbor. She wasn't nervous by nature, but life with her brothers had taught her that accidents could happen quickly, even when one wasn't taking chances.

Five minutes later, she pried a very warm corner brownie out of the pan, catching the part that gave way to gravity with her free hand and popping it into her mouth. She savored the warm gooey goodness as she went to the window. The sun was low, sending long shafts of light through the pines behind the trailer and bathing it in the golden glow of an early summer evening.

Troy opened the door, crossed to his truck like a man on a mission, pulled out some grocery bags from the back seat and returned to the trailer. The bed of the truck, which had held a number of boxes and duffels, was now empty. It appeared that Troy was almost done moving into his borrowed abode, which was a far cry from where he'd thought he'd be staying.

Kat looked at the remains of the brownie she held and then back at the trailer.

If anyone was in need of stress brownies, it was him. As things stood now, she was going to feel awkward on her own property because *he* felt awkward, and that wasn't going to fly. More importantly, she could not be left with an entire batch of brownies in a prolonged stressful situation. She no longer had neighbors to surprise with chocolate goodness, so in the name of self-preservation, she had to do something.

Kat waited until the pan was cool enough to handle and the brownies were firm enough not to droop, then she arranged most of them on a paper plate and lightly covered them with a paper towel.

"What's this?" Troy asked when she arrived at his open door after having taken the time to try to fix her curls so that she looked like a competent landlord and farm owner rather than someone who had just escaped from a burning hair salon.

"Housewarming." Caution shadowed his eyes, but he maintained a pleasant half smile. Barrier up. "*And*," she gave the word a healthy emphasis, "I thought we could spend a few minutes coming to an understanding."

"What kind of understanding?" His dark eyebrows came together as he spoke, but he stepped back, allowing her access to the trailer. It shifted a little under her weight, and when he closed the door, she realized just what a small space it was. And she was suddenly very much aware of…him.

Huh.

She set the brownies on the small counter next to the tiny sink and turned to face him, doing her best to appear nonchalant despite humming nerves.

"My family are good people," she said, deciding to dive into some background. "Honest people. Not like Arlie. He's our bad apple, I guess. Not *bad* bad, but…an opportunist."

"I'm experiencing that side of him now."

"Yes, you are." Kat let out a breath and smoothed the curls away from her face as she tried to untangle her thoughts. She didn't normally have a problem saying what she meant, but she also wasn't normally in a tiny space with a guy who was starting to put her nerves on edge.

She hadn't felt like this when they were outside or in her spacious kitchen, but in this trailer, she was having an attack of heightened awareness. The smell of brownies filled the air, but she could still catch his scent, something subtle and masculine that stirred things in her that had no business being stirred. She raised her gaze and forged on.

"I grew up wondering what far-out thing was going to hit the Farley family next. And for the sake of honesty, you should know that most of the stuff that happened was self-inflicted."

"I've watched your brother steer wrestle. Most guys drop from their horse. With James, it's like watching a cougar attack."

"Yes. That is how James goes through life. He springs at things. They all do—Andrew. Kent. James." She should have paused for a breath, but instead, she continued speaking, the words coming rapidly. "I wasn't a springer. I felt out of control for most of my life, but that was because I wanted to control things I couldn't. My family." Their finances. Their safety. Her brothers were forever looking for something to climb and then fall off of.

"That's hard to do."

He sounded like he spoke from experience.

"That didn't stop me from trying." She smiled a little. "An exercise in futility. So I decided to do things differently than my family. I chose a predictable, stable profession." He raised his eyebrows in a silent question, and she confessed to her less-than-thrilling career. "Bookkeeping."

"Do you like it?" There was surprise in his voice but no judgment.

"Actually…yes." Numbers made her happy. "But I met the wrong kind of people."

Again, his eyebrows went up, and despite everything, she sensed that he wanted to smile.

"My ex and I worked together."

"I assume your ex is the wrong kind of person?"

"It turned out that he is. In a way I didn't expect." She kept her tone light, refusing to hint at the bitterness that swamped her when she thought of Derek blithely planning to manipulate her into giving up her first refusal rights in regard to Littlegate Farm so that Dane could either snap up, or sell, the property.

Kat straightened her shoulders and got down to business. "The point is that I think things through." *With the exception of a major real estate purchase that had been all heart and very little head.* "I'm not like Arlie, and I'm not like my brothers. I consider consequences." *Usually.*

When she hesitated before coming to the meat of the matter, he gave her a *Go on* look.

"I'd like to rent you this trailer until you

find something better, and I don't expect to be paid until you're able to do so without doing harm to your bottom line."

Troy started to speak, but she raised a finger, effectively silencing him. "It's going to take you a while to recover from Arlie's fleecing, and I can wait for rent. But if you stay, you'll pay. Eventually." Except for the first and last month's rent, which he'd already paid her cousin, but they'd get to that part later.

"How do you know that it'll take a while to recover from the fleecing?"

"Will it?" she asked instead of explaining her reasoning.

"Possibly," he admitted. "I had a run of bad luck before Livia. And the lawyer for the custody thing was not cheap and… Yeah. It might take a month or two to get back on my feet." Troy rubbed his hand over the back of his neck before glancing at Livia, who was asleep in her carrier on the foldout bed. He studied her for a long moment and then turned back to Kat. "I'm in a spot," he said simply. The same words he'd spoken the night before, and they were just as true now as then.

"You are," she agreed.

He smiled a little at her solemn tone, making her wonder what it would take to make him smile a lot. She pushed the thought aside as his expression sobered.

"You don't have to decide tonight," she said before he could speak. "Think about it."

"Okay." He rubbed his neck. "I have a full day tomorrow. Can we talk in the morning?"

"Sure. When?"

"After breakfast. Say seven o'clock?"

"Done." She shifted her weight. This awkwardness-inducing trailer was way too small. "I'll…see you then."

"Sounds good."

Kat inched her way past him to the door, which he opened for her.

"Thank you for the brownies."

"You're welcome," she said after stepping out of the close confines. Once her feet hit gravel and she could smell pine instead of brownies, the claustrophobic effect of being in too close of quarters began to fade.

"Seven," she reiterated.

"Right." He gave her another half smile that didn't quite reach his eyes. "See you then."

CHAPTER THREE

"THE MAILBOX YOU'VE reached is full."

Troy's jaw muscles tightened at the automated voice message. How could a machine sound so smug? He set the phone aside and let out a frustrated breath.

Where are you, Arlie?

Troy was no stranger to tight spots, literally and figuratively, but now, with Livia, he couldn't tempt fate like he used to. There was too much at stake, so he needed to figure a way out of this situation as soon as possible.

It killed him that he was in it in the first place. Less than a year ago, he'd been kicking off what looked to be a stellar rodeo season. A moneymaker. Then came the injury, the expensive transmission replacement in his truck, the stunning revelation that he was about to be a father, the legal fees for the custody agreement he and Tiff had hammered out. Six weeks without a paycheck as he cared for his infant daughter.

His meager savings had evaporated despite him leaving rodeo midseason and going to work for Herm and Grace Michaels at Michaels Short Haul Trucking. Now he was between jobs in a borrowed trailer and indebted to a woman with wild hair and eyes the color of his favorite Wrangler shirt.

Troy adjusted his hand behind his head as he stared up at the ceiling of the small trailer. Not having a permanent home hadn't been a big deal until Livia was born and he'd discovered a protective instinct that he hadn't realized he possessed. When he'd attempted to explain the startlingly strong feelings to Saskia Belmont, his former rodeo travel partner, she'd told him she understood, but he didn't think she did. Mainly because he hadn't understood the strength of the parental bond himself until he'd held his little daughter in his arms.

Now everything centered around his kid and creating a secure existence for the two of them. Herm and Grace's decision to sell their trucking company had come as a shock, but with their recommendation, he'd landed the job with L&S Sand and Gravel. He just had to make enough shoeing horses during the busy summer months until the job started in September. All he needed was a roof over their heads, and thanks to Arlie, he'd thought he had one. Instead, he'd ended up in this predicament.

Had Arlie fleeced him on purpose? Or was he oblivious to the fact that the farm he'd rented out had been sold. Troy wanted to believe the latter. Arlie was a free-form kind of guy, but he hadn't seemed larcenous.

He'd find Arlie, get his money back, but until he managed to do that, he might have to swallow his pride and accept help—for Livia's sake.

"Anything for you, kid," he murmured to his sleeping daughter. He tried to smile after he spoke, but the corners of his mouth refused to move. He felt like he was failing her. Maybe it was best that he struggled while she was too young to be packing away memories of her dad needing to be dependent on others.

Livia stirred in her sleep. Troy tensed and then relaxed again when she sighed and settled.

He needed to focus on getting out of this mess, and that meant accepting Kat's offer. He'd stay and rent this trailer and pay her back once he was on his feet again financially. He hated being beholden, but there was that rock to his left and the hard spot to his right.

He'd tamp down his pride and do what he had to do. Troy Mackay didn't like owing people, and he was going to owe Kat Farley.

KAT SQUEEZED HER eyes tightly shut against the sunlight warming her face and then shot upright in bed. Sunlight?

Please don't be after seven.

Her phone wasn't on the nightstand, which made sense given that the last thing she remembered was starting yet another game of solitaire in the early morning hours. She beat the bedding around her until the phone bounced out of the blankets, and she groaned as she read the time. She had nine minutes to make herself presentable before the confab at seven.

After splashing water on her face and toweling it off, Kat tackled her curls. She wound them into a bun at the top of her head that she secured with a colorful scrunchie. She thought about makeup but figured that she'd screw something up if she hurried, so she headed to her closet instead. Jeans. Long-sleeve T-shirt advertising the local lumberyard. Good enough. She shrugged into a fleece vest, because the house was always cold upstairs and not much better downstairs.

The knock came just as she pulled a slipper out from under the bed. She batted around for the other, came up empty and decided stocking feet were fine.

"Coming," she called as Troy knocked again. She hurried across the living room and pulled the door open, taking a deep breath to counteract the adrenaline pumping through her body. "I overslept." And she'd forgotten how crazy attractive he was. Freaking cheekbones.

"Me too."

"What time did you wake up?" she asked, not believing him.

"Five thirty. Livia takes her bottle at five, so we both overslept."

She didn't bother trying to come up with a response to a seemingly sane person who thought that five thirty was oversleeping.

"I don't have the coffee on yet, but it shouldn't take long." She headed for the kitchen, assuming that Troy would follow, which he did. "Have a seat," she said, waving to the chair he'd occupied the previous day.

She put the coffee percolator together and set it on the burner.

"You don't see many percolators anymore." Troy shifted his daughter so that she was sitting on his lap. She immediately began patting the table in front of her.

"It works if there's a power outage." Kat couldn't help but smile as she watched the baby happily pounding on the table.

"Good point."

The baby let out a happy crow, and Troy brought his head close to hers to nuzzle her cheek. "What are you talking about, Button?"

Button.

Kat's heart squeezed.

The baby slapped the table and gave her dad a wide toothless smile. He planted a kiss on the side of her face, then went still, as if recalling that he and his daughter were not alone.

He glanced toward Kat, and she turned toward the coffee mugs a split second before their gazes met. Oh yeah. Her heart had just officially melted, and she couldn't decide if it was because of the open affection Troy showed his daughter or the way his cheeks warmed when he'd realized she was watching.

"Have you thought about my proposition?" She kept her attention on the coffeepot as if it needed watching.

"I have."

Kat chanced a casual glance as Troy shifted Livia on his lap. The little girl curled against him as she studied Kat. When Kat smiled, Livia buried her face in his shirt.

Troy patted the baby's back and gave Kat a nothing-personal half smile.

"Your cousin's behavior has nothing to do with you," Troy said, sounding as if he'd practiced the words. "You don't need to make it right."

Kat opened her mouth, but he stopped her by raising a finger, just as she'd done to him the night before.

"I'm just putting that out there before I accept your offer."

It took Kat a moment to realize she didn't have a fight on her hands. "That's…good."

"Unless you've had second thoughts?" The baby reached for his ear, but Troy didn't seem to notice, and Kat guessed from the shift in his expression that while he would accept her having second thoughts, it would be another blow he didn't need.

"I just thought you'd be a tougher sell," Kat said honestly.

"I can't afford to be."

Kat sensed that those were not easy words for him to say.

Troy shifted the baby on his lap again so she would let go out his earlobe. He tickled her belly, and she gave him a wide grin and snuggled against his chest. Kat realized that a sappy smile was starting to form on her face, so she turned toward the stove as the percolator began gurgling. When it stopped, she filled mugs and carried them to the table. "I don't have cream, but I do have sugar."

Troy waved a hand. "I'm good with un-adulterated caffeine."

"As am I," Kat said and sat. She brought the cup to her lips, taking care not to burn her mouth as she sucked in a tiny amount of the steaming liquid. Hot, hot, hot. She would not be mainlining caffeine for a while. Troy eyed the steam rising from his mug and pushed it farther away from the baby.

"I have to be more of a lukewarm guy now."

"Big life adjustments with a baby," she guessed.

Troy nodded and met her gaze. "Does it make you nervous renting to someone you don't know?"

Kat shrugged. "I googled you."

"Did you read about a rich kid doing dangerous things?"

"Didn't your parents worry?"

A choked laugh escaped his lips before he could stop it. "Um…no."

He left it at that, which gave Kat an inkling as to why he wasn't asking his parents for help.

"I also read about your rodeo career." He'd had a decent career, having made National Finals Rodeo three times. If she'd still followed rodeo, as she had in high school, she would have known his name.

"That's over, too. Elbow injury followed by fatherhood." He gave a self-deprecating smile. "That real-life thing, you know."

She pushed her cup to the side and clasped her hands in front of her, as she did when meeting with clients. The only problem was that the man sitting across the table was not one of her financial clients, dependent on her to keep his books organized. He was a hunky ex-rodeo rider with an adorable baby on his lap. A baby who was coyly flirting with her, smiling and then burying her face in her father's shirt.

"Just so you know," she said, dragging her attention away from the baby, "my brothers and I will hunt down Arlie and get your money back, so you don't owe me first and last month's rent. I'll get it." The last came out on a note of determination. When Arlie surfaced, he'd pay the money back, even if he had to do it in installments.

"That shouldn't be your job."

"Agreed. But I have three brothers scattered around the state, and you do not. My odds of collecting are better than yours."

He didn't answer, and Kat clasped her fingers a little harder. "There's always the option of calling the sheriff and reporting fraud."

He ran his thumb over the wooden tabletop next to his untouched coffee cup before lifting his gaze. "I'll get my money from Arlie, and I'll pay you for the time I stay here. All of it." He cleared his throat. "It might take me a couple of weeks to come up with the first month, but I will if you don't mind being patient."

"I just said I don't expect the first month's

rent, so it's not a question of patience." More like a question of pride. His pride.

He gave her a *We'll see* look but didn't push the matter. Kat, who was used to going head to head with obstinate brothers, had to stop herself from trying to settle things here and now.

"What was your plan of action if Arlie hadn't done what he did?" she asked. "I mean, can you continue as planned?"

"For the most part, yes." Before Kat could ask for clarification on "the most part," he continued, "I have to do some advertising, meet with the contacts Arlie gave me—if they actually exist," he added grimly. "Then I need to talk to the lady with the childcare center. Arlie said he could guarantee me six months on the farm—your farm, it turns out—and I hoped by that time to have found another place to live."

"I'll give you the six months." Before he could protest, she added, "I appreciate having someone here on the farm." She gave him a look. "Unless, of course, you're a nightmare tenant."

The beat of silence that followed told her she'd made an error, that the situation was too sensitive to joke about. Of course it was. Then a slow smile lifted the corners of Troy's mouth, and Kat's heart gave a double beat. This man was gorgeous.

"I'll try to behave, but I can't speak for my partner here."

Kat smiled because it was funny, but after her smile faded, she seemed incapable of tearing her gaze away from his. Troy reached for his coffee, breaking the spell. He drank too quickly but somehow got the steaming liquid down without coughing.

"I'm going to need some help around the place," Kat said, as if nothing had just happened, even though she was positive it had. "Not much, but every now and again—"

"It looks like you have a lot to do."

"Mmm." Kat made a noncommittal noise, even though he'd spoken the truth. There was so much to do, but she didn't want him to feel like he was about to become her full-time handyman.

"I'll give you whatever time you need," he said. "What are your plans for the place?"

"To restore it to what it once was." She sipped her coffee. To what she remembered as a kid. A calm, almost pastoral place. The antithesis of the rowdy Farley Ranch. Not that she couldn't handle rowdiness. She held her own quite nicely, if necessary—the key words being "if necessary." She just liked her rowdiness in small doses.

"Which was...?"

"My aunt and uncle raised Morgan horses, and after my uncle passed away, my aunt sold the Morgans and began boarding horses. Between the hay she raised and the boarding, the farm paid for itself." She dipped her chin as she looked at him. "Boarding pays better than raising horses. For a while, this place was a little gold mine, but then my aunt got older and had trouble feeding the horses, and Arlie was off being Arlie. She owned the farm outright, so she leased out the hay farming and retired."

Now the fences were all either down or sagging, meaning Kat had some work ahead of her to get the place back to being the horse haven that would help her with the mortgage payments.

"And you bought the place from your aunt."

"She broke her hip last fall and went into assisted living while she recovered. She came to find out she liked it. She made friends and took part in activities, which I guess she missed living here alone. She decided to sell Littlegate to finance her apartment in the facility, and she wanted to keep the farm in the family." Kat smiled reminiscently. "When I was twelve or thirteen, I made her promise to give me first crack at the place if she ever let it go. She did."

"Lucky that you were in a position to afford it."

She met his gaze. "I had to sell all of my cows to do it."

Like many former ranch kids, she still owned animals in the family herd, paid her share of the expenses and labor, and every year, when the yearlings sold, they provided her with a nice chunk of change to either invest or save. To come up with the down payment for Littlegate, she'd had to liquidate her portion of the herd. She'd also liquidated her investment account, which left her with a teensy cushion of savings.

Troy cocked his head, and she instantly regretted mentioning the cows after telling him she was in no hurry for rent.

"Some of my bookkeeping clients chose to stay with me after I quit my firm. I'm doing okay." As long as nothing blew up in her face. "The difficulty was quickly putting things together so that my aunt could get the money she needed. I'll start replacing my cows next year."

"I see."

Kat wondered what exactly he saw. The little holes in her story concerning finances, which were fine as long as she didn't encounter anything wildly unexpected? Which she knew was a stretch for a Farley.

They lifted their coffee cups at the same time, and that was when Kat noticed the baby's eyes had closed.

"She's asleep," Kat silently mouthed.

The baby's eyes popped open.

"Just faking me out," Troy replied, stroking her head with his free hand before meeting Kat's gaze. "I don't know if I've said this yet, but thanks for letting us stay."

Once again, she had a hard time tearing her eyes away from his, but that was something she was going to have to learn to live with. There were worse things than having a hot cowboy on the premises. She just needed to stay out of the trailer, the small confines of which amplified awareness.

She lifted her cup in a small salute, doing her best to appear as if she weren't cataloging the things about him that made her take notice. She lifted the corners of her mouth into an easy smile totally at odds with her humming nerves.

"I'm glad you're staying."

WITHIN HALF AN hour after meeting with Kat, Troy had fed Livia, changed her and was on his way to Larkspur, driven by a deep desire to set his life right.

Three days ago, he'd believed that he was about to start building his new life. He was doing that, but with more obstacles to overcome than he'd first anticipated.

If it hadn't been for Kat Farley's generosity, he'd be in deep mud right now, and he couldn't stop thinking about just how deep.

He knew he was lucky…but there was also the fact that his new landlady was too attractive for his peace of mind. That wild hair, those eyes. Oh yeah. Back in the day, he would have totally made a move in her direction, but that was not an option now. After the fiasco that had been his marriage to Tiff and the arrival of Livia, he was not in the market for complications. Kat Farley was his landlady.

His much-needed landlady.

His position was precarious, and he was not about to screw things up.

The Larkspur city limits sign was set a good half a mile from the first buildings in town—a grocery store and gas station. The town founders had been optimistic, but given the way that Montana was growing, their optimism could pay off.

Troy pulled up to a fuel pump, and while he filled the tank, he debated his first stop. Daycare or business center?

Daycare. Livia came first. After that,

he'd see about printing some advertising for bulletin boards around town. Then he'd touch base with L&S Sand and Gravel to let them know he was in the area in case something came up. Maybe the guy he was replacing would retire early, or they might need substitute drivers. Once he'd done all of that, he'd call the two potential shoeing clients whose names Arlie had given him. He hoped they were real. If not, he'd be back to square one, which was becoming a familiar trip.

Livia stirred as he got back into the truck with the receipt in hand. Her eyes fluttered and opened.

"Here's the plan, Button. Daycare, printer, a couple of cold calls, the grocery store and then back to the farm where you get lunch." If she didn't need it sooner. He had a bottle in the travel bag. "What do you think?"

A howl filled the cab of the truck, and Troy let out a sigh as he put the rig in gear. Sometimes a person felt like letting it all out, and a part of him envied his daughter's ability to do just that.

Daisy Lane Daycare was the only licensed childcare facility in Larkspur, Montana, which wasn't surprising given that the population hovered around the two thousand mark. Troy followed the GPS through the rather charming town, the main street of which still boasted original brick buildings and storefronts. Old elms lined the street, and halfway down Main, he'd stopped to allow an older woman with two small dogs in her arms to jaywalk in front of him. She smiled pleasantly and nodded. He nodded back. Friendly town.

Livia had quieted by the time he parked across the street from a bungalow painted pale blue with white trim. There was a daisy-shaped sign at the gate that read, "Daisy Lane. Children blossom here." But daffodils rather than daisies swayed in the breeze as he carried Livia to the gate. An omen? He hoped not.

His equine nemesis was named Daffodil. Last August, he'd almost made rodeo history by becoming the first guy to successfully ride her twice, but she'd gotten the better of him a fraction of a second before the buzzer. Ended his career.

Granted, fatherhood would have ended his career if she hadn't. While he hadn't gone out in a blaze of glory, it had been a memorable ride, one that people still brought up from time to time. Not that he spent much time around the rodeo crowd anymore. He missed it, but he was on a more important mission now.

A petite young woman with a blue kerchief holding back her shoulder-length red hair answered the door, giving him a polite but cautious look.

"I'm Troy Mackay. This is Livia, my daughter." Livia immediately pressed her face against his shoulder.

"Yes. Livia will be joining us in September." She held the door a little wider. "I'm Daisy."

The Daisy he'd envisioned in their phone conversation and subsequent emails had been an older woman.

"Hi, sweetie," Daisy said to Livia, who peeked at the woman before once again burying her face. "Have you come to look around?" she asked Troy. "If so, we'll need to set something up. I only give tours when the children aren't here."

Safety. He liked that.

"Actually, I wanted to touch base and to discuss your drop-in policy. I'm going to start shoeing horses, and you said something about drop-in's being welcome?"

Her expression clouded. "I have openings for three drop-ins a day and those slots are snapped up fast. Parents with appointments, things like that."

"You're saying—"

"It's a crapshoot," she said candidly. "To be safe, I'd book a week out."

"I can do that."

"Unless you want to book for next week. I'm full up."

"Then I guess I'd better make a schedule and book two weeks ahead."

"That would be safest."

Livia turned her head to study the woman who smiled warmly in return. A second later, Livia smiled back and then buried her face again.

"Would you like to book a tour?" Daisy asked.

"When I know my schedule, yes, I would. I'll call you."

"Looking forward to it."

Troy retraced his path past the daffodils and through the gate. Okay. Childcare wouldn't be a slam dunk. He'd have to do some careful scheduling.

Livia cooed at him when he buckled her back into her seat and then started playing with the colorful stuffed animals attached to the handle of the carrier. So far, so good moodwise, but that could change in a nanosecond.

As could many things in life.

He tickled his baby. She laughed, and his world was brighter.

CHAPTER FOUR

KAT'S EYES WIDENED as the server at the Homestead Diner set a ginormous salad in front of her friend Maddie Kincaid. "Yowza," she said softly.

Whitney Fox's forehead furrowed as she studied the vat of greens. "That's practically a full harvest."

"What?" Maddie raised her fork. "I'll take the leftovers in a doggie bag, because I probably won't get away from the shop until well after dinnertime."

Her client had rescheduled a wedding-dress fitting to late afternoon, so Maddie was able to meet with Whitney and Kat after all, but she'd be working late because of it.

"It's just so much…health," Kat said as a plate of fries was placed in front of her. Girls lunch out had always been about reveling in really bad food choices.

"Fries go soggy. Not my idea of a good leftover dinner eaten between fittings," Maddie said. She dipped a carrot in the dressing at the side of her plate. "So you honestly never heard of Troy Mackay?" Of course, the first subject of conversation was Kat's cowboy and his baby.

"I quit following rodeo years ago," Kat replied.

Maddie, on the other hand, had barrel-raced until her schedule became too crazy to continue competing in an expensive and time-consuming hobby. She still followed rodeo and was vocal about her desire to go back to barrel racing someday.

"He—" Maddie gestured with the carrot, "—is one of three guys to successfully ride Daffodil." She bit off the end of the carrot before explaining. "Bronc of the Year for four years in a row. Your cowboy came this close to being the first person to ride her twice last summer, but he came off just before the buzzer. Got hung up in the rigging." She reached for one of Kat's fry. "It was ugly."

"I read about his injury." Kat glanced at

Whitney. "I suppose you're familiar with him, too?"

"I've heard of him, but I haven't been to a rodeo in two years." Whit pushed her long blond hair behind one ear. "I might have paid more attention if I'd known what he looked like. Not that I spent a lot of time perusing his images on the internet after your texts, or anything like that."

"I, too, did not do that," Maddie said solemnly.

"He's a looker," Kat agreed. And he smelled terrific and made her nerves go on high alert. She found the guy fascinating, and nothing exacerbated fascination like dwelling on it. Or trying to stop it. So she was simply going to let it run its course and not overthink things.

"He doesn't share custody?" Maddie asked.

"I don't know the ins and outs, but apparently, the mother relinquished custody, and Troy is on his own with the baby." Kat picked up a fry and ate it without bothering with ketchup. "The guy's in a rough spot."

Whitney raised a warning eyebrow, and Kat let out a breath.

"I'm not trying to rescue him. Those days are gone." As the oldest and most consequence-aware Farley sibling, Kat had spent too much time trying to manage her wayward brothers or rescue them when she couldn't talk them out of whatever. She'd finally learned that she couldn't save people from themselves, but she could certainly run herself ragged trying.

"I'd rescue him," Maddie said.

"Okay... I might, too." Whitney shot Kat a wry smile before her expression sobered. "And I think it might be good for you to have someone on the farm with you. Heavy lifting and all that."

"I like that part," Kat admitted. "I've got some challenges ahead if I'm going to start boarding horses again." Boarding, coupled with her day job, would allow her to pay for the repairs and maintenance of the long-neglected farm. But before she could advertise, she needed to have the fences and feeding facilities in tip-top shape. For that, she needed help. And possibly some luck.

Materials were expensive, and she was still getting a handle on a tenuous budget. She'd told Troy that she didn't need money right now, and that was correct…but she was going to need the farm to pay for itself soon.

"How soon do you hope to advertise?"

"Yesterday?" Kat shrugged. "The sooner I have some income streaming in from the place, the better." The three sat in thoughtful silence for a moment, then Kat said, "I may have jumped into buying the farm too quickly." She bit her lip. "I regret nothing, though." It had felt so good to take Derek down a notch. How could she regret that? If Dane had gotten hold of the property, she'd bet dollars to donuts that he would have cut it up and sold it off in tiny parcels. She wasn't about to let that happen.

"It was quick," Whit agreed. "But it was a sweet deal. I don't see how you could have walked away. Well," she amended, "I do, but I'm glad you didn't." She reached out to touch Kat's arm. "There's such a thing as playing it too safe. You weren't meant to live the buttoned-down life you made for yourself."

Maddie nodded in agreement. "It'd be one thing if you were happy."

"You don't think I was happy?"

"I think you were…satisfied. You did what you set out to do," Maddie said diplomatically.

"You weren't *happy* happy." Whit cocked her head as she studied Kat in a thoughtful way. "It was like you were wearing a sweater that didn't fit right, but you'd convinced yourself it was fine because it was warm."

Kat smiled ruefully at the imagery. "I think Aunt Margo might have figured that out, too. Or maybe she just remembered me insisting that I wanted to live on her farm someday."

Kat had always loved Littlegate. When she was a kid, she'd told Margo more than once that she never wanted to leave. Of course, back then the farm was more than hay meadows. In addition to the beautiful Morgan horses, there'd been goats and sheep and a couple of cows that Margo kept just because. Dozens of chickens and ducks waddled here and there, and for a time, there'd been beehives.

The Farley Ranch didn't lack for animals or things to do, but there was a peace about Littlegate Farm that spoke to Kat when she visited. There was rhythm to the day that was never disrupted by a quick trip to the hospital to set a broken bone. Ironically, Arlie had always been more at home on her ranch than on his family farm. More action there.

"Blood will tell," Maddie said before sipping her iced tea. Kat gave her a curious look, and Maddie dapped the moisture from her lips. "You bought a farm on a dare, installed a hunky cowboy and, as far as we know, haven't made a single spreadsheet. That's pretty close to going full Farley." She raised her eyebrows to emphasis her point.

"That's kind of scary," Kat said, only half kidding. "If you see me on the roof with a makeshift parachute, stage an intervention, okay?"

Actually, she was going onto the roof

later that day to tack down loose shingles before the next rainstorm hit, but unlike her younger brothers, she intended to use a ladder rather than gravity to return to solid ground.

Maddie's phone buzzed, and she muttered, "What now?" as she dug in her purse. Whit and Kat exchanged glances.

Maddie had always been the easiest going of the three of them, but she was starting to look a little frayed around the edges. Even her dark hair was twisted into a messy bun at the back of her head instead of swinging in the silky curtain that Kat envied and had spent too much time trying to emulate.

Once she answered the phone, Maddie spoke briefly, saying, "I understand, and I'll be right there." She dropped the phone back into her purse. "Delivery problem."

"Do you want us to have your salad boxed? We'll drop it off."

"Thank you!" She scooted out of the booth seat and hefted her overly large purse. "Call if you need me," she said to Kat. She eyed Whit's fries and added, "If you guys have extra fries you don't want, send them along, too."

"What about the soggy factor?" Kat asked innocently.

"I'll suck it up and deal with it."

"Should we be worried?" Kat asked Whit after Maddie started for the door and then came back for her phone, which was still on the table, half covered by her napkin.

"I don't think so. Not yet, anyway."

They requested a box for the salad, and as they waited for the server to return, Whit said, "I know you're busy, but if you have a little extra time on Sunday…"

Kat brightened. "Horseback ride?"

"Kind of. I told my dad I would fix the north boundary fence before I head back to Missoula so that he can turn out the yearling heifers, and I wouldn't mind some company." She gave Kat a hopeful smile. "I'd be happy to help you tackle some project in the near future in return. I'm sure you have a few in the queue."

"I'm happy to help," Kat said. "I take it your dad is still on the crutches after the knee surgery?"

"Only a cane now, but he's not mobile enough to fix the fence, and Manuel is visiting his family in Arizona. New granddaughter." Whit glanced down at the table and then back up at Kat. "I'm glad you bought your farm."

"Me too," Kat said slowly. She had fears, but no regrets. "You guys are right. I built a life that I expected to be fulfilling and worry-free, and I hated it." And she'd dated a guy she thought she could build a life with only to find out that she had misread him.

"Some things we have to learn firsthand. You weren't meant to have a milquetoast life."

"I agree. I'm concerned about whether I can make the farm pay for itself, but... I'm a Farley. Things will work out in the end."

Kat repeated the words to herself as she headed to her car parked four blocks from the Homestead Café. Whit had agreed to drop the boxed-up salad and fries at Maddie's western bridal boutique before stopping at the post office two doors down.

Things will work out, she repeated again

as she walked past Cashman Properties. She allowed herself a quick glance through the spotless windows into the office, but there was no sign of Dane Cashman, and she felt a whisper of relief, which in turn made her mouth tighten.

Stop letting the Cashmans dictate your feelings.

Eventually, she would bump into the man—that was a given, considering the size of Larkspur—but losing out on properties was part of the game in real estate, and she had no reason to believe he held a grudge. He'd wanted Littlegate Farm, and Derek had been so certain that he could talk her into passing on the deal that he'd guaranteed his brother the farm was his. It wasn't. Never would be.

She'd won, and now she had to make sure she didn't lose it. That required putting Littlegate Farm back into a position where it could pay for itself.

"Kat."

She stopped dead at the sound of her name, her stomach lurching in the instant before she realized it wasn't Derek who'd called out. It was his brother.

"Dane?" She turned to give him a polite look as he closed the space between them. He'd apparently been walking not far behind her.

"Do you have a few minutes?"

"I really don't," she said, pushing her curls back. Dane's gaze followed the motion of her hand, and she realized that he'd probably never seen the natural state of her hair.

Drink it in, buddy.

Dane gave his smile a little extra oomph when she pointedly raised her eyebrows. He was taller and more classically handsome than his older brother, and he had a charming self-deprecating attitude that hid a Kansas-sized sense of entitlement. Classic baby of the family.

The baby of the family shouldn't be tying her stomach in a knot, but he had made a low-level threat to her via his brother—that she was in over her head and was going to regret buying the farm out from under him.

Probably heat-of-the-moment stuff, but it didn't endear him to her.

His smile faded after she refused to play the game and smile back. "I think we should talk."

She was not going down that rabbit hole. "We have nothing to discuss, Dane. Personally. Professionally. I have to go."

If she and Derek hadn't had such a blowup before parting ways, she might have heard his brother out. But when she heard Dane's voice, she heard Derek's, and she wasn't ready to deal with either of them.

"Don't be this way, Kat."

Kat recognized an order when she heard one, despite the mild tone, and it was all she could do not to tell him that she'd *be* any way she chose to be. She was no longer "compliant."

"I have to go, Dane."

She turned on her heel, got into her car and maneuvered it out of the tight space despite her jangling nerves. As she pulled into the lane, she saw him turn toward his office.

Go sell a house, Dane. Leave me alone.

TROY'S LAST STOP before heading back to the camp trailer was at his future place of employment.

The yards of L&S Sand and Gravel were located two miles north of Larkspur on a spur off the county road aptly named Dirt Road. He waited for a truck and pup loaded with road gravel to turn out of the yard in front of him before passing through the gates and parking beside an older double-wide that served as the offices.

He'd fed Livia shortly after the visit to the printers, and she'd started rubbing her eyes on the drive to L&S, a sure sign that sleep was near. That said, leaving her in her car seat was not an option, so he gently unhooked the seat and carried it with him.

"Hello?" an older lady in a leopard top said from behind her desk as Troy awkwardly made his way into the office.

"Hi. I'm Troy Mackay."

"Mr. Mackay." The woman rose to her feet and came to the counter. "I'm Louise. We spoke during the interview."

Yes, they had. Like Michaels Short Haul Trucking, L&S Sand and Gravel was a husband-and-wife affair. During the phone interview, Troy had spoken to both Louise and Sam Fletcher.

"Hon, it's so good to meet you in person, and you brought the baby."

Troy held his breath, but for once, Livia didn't do her stranger-danger thing. She was too fascinated by Louise's sparkling earrings and the little gold clips in her almost purple hair.

"Aren't you just precious?" Louise shifted her attention back to Troy. "Have you found a place to live?"

"I have," he said without a trace of irony. "I thought I'd stop by to say hello and to tell you that if you need a substitute driver at any time, I'm here. If you don't, I'll see you in September."

Louise touched his sleeve. "That's very thoughtful of you." Her expression clouded. "You do understand why we have no official start date for you, right?"

"As long as I can start before winter, I'll be okay." People didn't have much need for farriers once the weather turned and shoes were pulled until spring.

"Bobby is hot to retire," Louise assured him, "but until he gets his medical stuff taken care of, he needs the insurance. Poor thing. He thought he was going to retire a week ago, then the doctor come up with that heart thing, and… You're a good sport for putting off your start date."

"I'm just happy to have a job waiting for me."

"I hear that you shoe horses."

"I do."

"Are you busy?"

"Hope to be soon."

"Good." Louise made a show of fanning her face in relief. "We'd hate to lose you after all the nice things Grace and Herm shared with us. Now let me make certain I have all your contact information." She went to her computer and tapped a few keys, then read his phone number to him.

"That's it."

"And do you have an address?"

"It's temporary. I'm looking for something more permanent if you hear of anything."

The look Louise gave him before focusing back on the computer screen made his stomach tighten.

"Not many rentals?"

"Maybe in September. The summer people fill up everything else. We're too close to many nice rivers." She looked up again. "You may as well give me your temporary address. You may be there longer than you think."

"That would be 5530 Crescent Mountain Road."

Louise looked up again. "Are you staying at the Bealman place?"

"No. Littlegate Farm."

"Are you caretaking for Margo? I heard a rumor that she may not be coming back anytime soon."

Troy chose his words carefully, not knowing the dynamics of the community or what information Kat wanted out there. "Her niece is in the main house. I'm renting a trailer there."

"Huh. Interesting. I didn't realize that Kat was back. Last I heard she had a job in Spokane."

"She's back."

"Are you friends?"

Troy took a moment. "Her brother and I met through rodeo."

Louise's eyes widened. "You are the first bona fide rodeo star we've had work here."

"I don't know about *star*," he said.

"Will you be competing in the Larkspur Days Rodeo? There's still time to sign up. Sam is on the board."

Troy nodded at Livia. "I'm afraid those days are done. I'm on a new adventure now."

"The best kind," Louise said, playfully taking hold of Livia's little foot. Livia gave the woman a wide smile and then squealed happily as she reached for an earring. Louise expertly moved the bauble out of range before beaming at Troy's baby from a safe distance.

"We're glad to have you, Troy. Herm and Grace spoke so highly of you. Plus…you're a rodeo star."

Troy smiled gamely.

"Well, I have all your information, and if I'm in need of a sub, I'll give you a call."

"Thanks, Louise." He lifted the carrier

off the counter. "I—we—appreciate it. The only thing is that I have to work around childcare, so the more notice, the better."

"Gotcha." She pointed a finger at him and went back to her desk as Troy headed for the exit.

"Hey," he said before he opened the door. "Do you know where Arlie Stokes might be working now?" It was a long shot.

Louise gave a merry laugh. "Not in this area, that's for sure. Arlie burned a few bridges. He's a charmer, but not very dependable."

Troy simply smiled rather than explain how familiar he was with Arlie's character flaws. Small towns were no place to drop an opinion too soon—not even to someone who seemed to share your sentiments.

"Thanks, Louise." He touched a finger to his ball cap. "I'll see you soon."

KAT WAS ON the roof of her house with a hammer in one hand when Troy drove into Littlegate Farm. She straightened as he drove past the house, gave a wave and then went back to what she was doing. Troy parked next to the trailer, shooting another quick look toward the house as he got out of the truck. Kat had disappeared, but he could hear the tap of a hammer from the opposite side of the roof, which meant that she hadn't hit the ground.

He opened the back door, unfastened Livia's car seat and carefully pulled it out without waking her. The tapping continued as he headed to the trailer. Under normal circumstances, he would have offered to lend a hand, but right now, his hands were officially full. He had his baby and groceries to unload. There were also two propane bottles in the back of his truck wedged in next to the forge and his shoeing equipment.

Livia woke up as soon as he set the carrier on the bench, so he quickly put away the groceries, fed her, changed her and finally set her on the blanket on the floor to get a little exercise. She wasn't quite crawling, but she was so close, pushing herself up onto her hands and knees and rocking. Troy was in no hurry to see her grow up, but milestones were exciting.

"Atta girl, Button," he said as she did a few baby pushups. She gave him a drooly grin, and he smiled back before taking her formula-stained sweatshirt and dropping it into the plastic bin he used as a hamper. They were both running out of clothes, and he would need to make a trip to the Laundromat in Larkspur within the next day or two. Or would he? He stepped into the kitchen and regarded the micro sink, debating his handwashing skills when a strangled scream brought his head up.

Kat.

Heart pounding, he scooped up Livia with one hand and wretched the door open with the other. It didn't take long to circumnavigate the house. Nothing. The ladder was still standing. No tools on the ground and definitely no landlady. That was when he heard the front door scrape open. He reversed course and found a white-faced Kat standing on the porch, her arms wrapped around her middle.

"I know what's in the attic," she said in a dazed voice.

"How... You didn't fall off the roof?"

"Off the roof?" She gave him a quizzical look. "No."

It was only when his palm touched the soft cotton of her long-sleeved T-shirt that Troy realized he'd reached out to touch her, to reassure himself that she was okay and to maybe do the same for her. She responded with a rueful half smile as he dropped his hand.

"I'm fine," she said. "I heard the noises in the attic while I was patching the loose shingles, so I thought I'd go inside and lift the attic trapdoor a few inches and see what it was."

"And…"

"It flew at me."

"Bat?"

She shook her head. "I'm pretty sure it's an owl. Whatever it is, it's big, and it's getting in through the broken gable vent. There's probably just enough room to ease through." She rubbed her hands over her arms again.

"Are you sure that you're okay?"

She muttered something about being a

Farley and then straightened her shoulders. "I'm fine. The light fixture, not so much."

"The light fixture?"

She motioned for him to follow her into the house. A stepladder lay on its side beneath the attic trapdoor, a flashlight and a broken sconce beside it.

"I didn't fall," she explained quickly. "I landed on my feet, but I knocked the ladder over and it hit the fixture."

Troy had no words.

"I know," Kat said, pushing her curls back from her forehead. "It could have been bad, but how was I supposed to know the thing would come at me?"

"She might have babies," Troy guessed, shifting Livia in his arms. She reached for Kat, who held out a finger for her to grab. Livia pulled Kat's hand closer, her little fist death-gripping Kat's index finger.

"Oh, I'd say she does, which means we won't be chasing her out anytime soon." Kat smiled at Livia and then glanced at Troy and frowned. "Are *you* okay?"

"Now that I know you didn't fall off the roof, yes."

"Sorry."

"You know, you probably shouldn't do roof repairs when you're alone."

"Maybe not," she conceded, gently pulling her finger out of Livia's tight baby grip. "But there's water damage showing on the upstairs ceilings, and with storms forecasted in the next few days, I thought I might as well start putting the place right."

"My first broken bone came from falling off a roof, so I'm respectful."

"I've seen pictures of you parasailing off cliffs," she said dryly.

"I'm more safety-oriented now." His hold on Livia tightened. The thought of her doing some of the things he'd done unnerved him.

"Except for that rodeo thing?"

His silence probably answered the question, but he clarified. "I'm done with rodeo. Priorities shift when you have a kid."

"Do you miss it?"

"It was my life for a long time. Yeah, I do miss it, but…" He gave Livia a quick kiss on her head. "Life is all about trade-offs."

She gave him an odd look. "It is." She

took a backward step. "Anyway, I'm fine, the light is not. You probably have a lot to do, so…"

I've been dismissed.

He'd take it. He did have a lot to do, but as he headed back to the trailer, baby in his arms, he couldn't shake the what-ifs. What if Kat had hurt herself in the owl attack? He had enough worry on his hands with Livia without adding his landlady to the mix.

Surprisingly, Arlie's contacts had both been legit. One was the ex-wife of a fellow trucker. She'd come into some money and raised Arabian horses as a hobby. The other was a guy with an ornery stud that was a challenge to shoe. According to the Arabian owner, whom he contacted first, the stud guy couldn't hold on to a farrier, but he refused to part with his horse. The stud owner said that the Arabian lady's horses were pampered and undisciplined, and she couldn't keep a farrier, either.

Not the most auspicious way to begin his career, but Troy booked them both for appointments the following day. He would take what he could get as he started building clientele. Unfortunately, neither had heard from Arlie in a very long time, and they were no help in trying to pin down the guy's location.

He'd surface eventually, and Troy would get his money back. When the summer people left Larkspur, he and Livia would move to a place where he paid rent every month and wasn't beholden to anyone.

Although, he was kind of concerned about who would keep an eye on Kat then as she scampered across roof tops and did battle with mama owls.

KAT SWEPT UP the glass of the broken light sconce, replaced the bulb in the now naked fixture and hauled the step ladder to the screened-in back porch. Her nerves had finally calmed from the close encounter with the flying menace in the attic, and she had to admit that Troy made an excellent point about not getting onto roofs—or ladders—while she was alone on the farm.

You're not alone now.

She was not, and she hadn't finished

tacking down the shingles. Curiosity had also gotten the better of her, and she'd decided to take a peek in the attic.

You're a Farley, and when a Farley falls off a ladder, they get right back on.

Besides that, the hammer and tacks were still up there where she'd left them, and they needed to be retrieved.

Sucking in a breath, Kat started up the ladder that leaned against the back side of the house, out of view of the camp trailer. She didn't have a problem with heights, but hitting the floor today made her cautious, and she was glad that Troy couldn't see how slowly she was climbing. Finally, she stepped onto the roof, and after moving a healthy way away from the edge, she stood with her hands on her hips reacclimating herself. She was fine. The view was lovely, and she could finish with the shingles.

To the north, she could see the Bealman property, a gem of a place surrounded on three sides by federal land. Unlike Littlegate Farm, that property had been well maintained even after the elderly owners had moved. A nephew had lived there for a spell, but now there was only a caretaker whose name Kat didn't know. He was a nice guy who'd helped Margo with chores around her place when Arlie wasn't here. In other words, a guy who helped Margo often.

It took less than fifteen minutes for Kat to finish tacking down the shingles. She'd tar over the nails in the next day or two, but for now, things were better than they had been. If all went well, the water stains on the bedroom and kitchen ceilings would not get any larger.

She went to the edge of the roof to drop the hammer to the ground and nearly had a heart attack when she saw Troy standing at the bottom of the ladder.

"Make some noise in the future," she said. "I could have killed you." She made a point of tossing the hammer several yards away from him.

"I heard you hammering again. Livia's asleep, so I thought I'd see if you need a hand."

"I'm done for now." She picked up the nail can and made her way to the ladder.

Troy held one edge as she climbed down and stepped back when she reached the bottom rungs.

"You know, I'm actually good on ladders."

"As you demonstrated earlier today?"

"That was a fluke."

"An owl attack? You call that a fluke?" He gave her a disbelieving look.

"Right. What was I thinking?" She tilted her head to one side. "I'm making hot dogs for dinner. Would you and Livia like to come over?" She wasn't sure where the invitation had come from, but once voiced, it felt right.

Troy looked like he was going to decline, so she was surprised when he said yes.

"Is everything okay?" he added.

"Fine. I just don't feel like eating alone." She smiled a little at his skeptical look. "Don't worry. I won't make a habit of inviting you for hot dogs."

She wanted him to know that there wouldn't be a steady stream of invites. He might be living a stone's throw away from her house, but they were separate entities with separate lives.

"Then I won't make a habit of asking if I can use your washing machine. Liv is getting low on clothes, and I haven't had time to hit a coin-op laundry."

"Of course you can use my machine. Anytime."

He gave her one of his *We'll see* looks, which in turn made her want to take him by the front of his shirt and shake him. Someday, she'd love to sit him down and discuss what had happened to make him so freaking independent. Or maybe he'd just been born that way.

"I need to check on Liv. What time for dogs?"

"Five?"

"That was ten minutes ago."

Kat laughed. It felt good not knowing what time it was.

"Let's make it six," she said.

Troy smiled, and a bubble of warmth rose in her, which in turn triggered a red flag. She wasn't doing bubbles of warmth with her tenant…but she wasn't sure what to do to stop it. Retract the invitation? Keep her distance?

Or perhaps she could enjoy the feeling, secure in the knowledge that she was never letting herself get conned by a man again? If there was one thing Kat was good at, it was self-discipline—impulse purchase of a farm notwithstanding.

She had this.

Troy wasn't much of a wine drinker, possibly because Myra and Daniel, his parents, had been such wine snobs, but the mellow red that Kat served with the hot dogs was very drinkable. When she held up the bottle, he pushed his empty glass forward, and Kat poured him a refill.

Livia had nodded off, cradled in the crook of one of his arms, which was now going to sleep. He took a chance and carefully settled her in her carrier. She sighed, but her eyes stayed closed.

"Success?"

Troy smiled. "Appears so. For now anyway."

The washing machine began its spin cycle

in the next room, and soon it would be time to transfer everything to the dryer. Kat had been nonplussed at the way he'd thrown everything into one load in the old top-loading machine, but he wasn't picky about his clothes, and Livia's were essentially disposable, as she would soon outgrow them.

He sipped his wine as the washer shook the house. They'd been discussing his childcare issues.

"There's nothing wrong with asking for help, you know," Kat said. "Worst-case scenario, the person you ask says no."

Logically, he knew that, but it didn't make it any easier for him to reach out when he needed assistance.

"I've always handled things on my own."

"But you're not on your own."

"No." He was not, and he had the pins and needles in his arm from holding his baby in an awkward position to prove it.

"All I'm saying is that I have experience with kids, and if you need an emergency sitter, I'll help. The beauty of working remotely is that I can set my own hours, which frees me up for other things."

Like putting her farm back together. As he saw it, Kat was going to be one busy woman.

"I appreciate the offer."

Kat's lips curved as she slowly shook her head, giving him the feeling that she'd understood the thought going through his head was that he already owed her too much and didn't want to add babysitting to the mix.

Troy's first two clients had both asked him to come ASAP, which was definitely a red flag. It probably meant that they'd worked their way through the other farriers in the area, but he couldn't afford to be picky. If it had four feet and needed to be trimmed or shod, he would get the job done.

He'd explained that he didn't have childcare on the weekend or for the coming week, but neither potential client had seen that as an issue. They'd told him to bring the child along.

Troy had decided that he could do that. Livia would fall asleep on the drive and hopefully either continue to sleep or entertain herself with her carrier toys. If she cried, he'd take a break.

Not ideal but doable, and both clients had been insistent. They wanted him before he was booked solid, so he'd put aside his misgivings and agreed to see Patricia Knox and her Arabians on Sunday morning. He'd visit Walt Stenson and his stud in the early afternoon. Sunday also happened to be the day that Kat was helping a friend.

A rustling sounded overhead, and Kat shook her head again, eyes on her wine.

"I'm just going to let that be," she said.

Troy gave a small laugh and focused on his wine. The washing machine had stopped spinning. He needed to get his clothes into the dryer so that he could head back to the camp trailer. He figured he could pick them up in the morning if Kat didn't need the machine.

He was about to get out of his chair when another sound above his head caught his attention. Rain.

"Guess you got the roof done in the nick of time."

"For now. I still have to tar, but I'm sure having the shingles in place helps."

"Have you done a lot of roofing?" He couldn't think of anyone he knew who'd fixed a roof.

"My share. We all pitched in on the ranch, and frankly, no one wanted my brothers on roofs." Kat leaned her elbows on the table, a thoughtful expression on her face. "You know, that might be a good pickup line." She lowered her voice. "Hey, sweet thang. Ever done any roofing?"

Troy grinned and swirled his wine. "You'll have to tell me how it goes if you use it."

"Not me," she said. "I was offering it to you."

"I already have a woman in my life," he pointed out, tilting his head in the direction of the baby carrier.

"No room for another?" The words had barely left her lips when Kat held up a hand, palm toward him. "I didn't just say that. None of my business."

He didn't correct her, but the low-level

vibe that had hummed between them during dinner had just intensified.

Time to go.

The washer slowed to a stop, and he pushed his chair back.

This slow-burn attraction to Kat, which was unlike anything he'd experienced before, was starting to feel dangerous. With Tiff, he'd experienced white-hot heat. They'd been wild for one another, but ultimately, the cliché had been proven true. Hot flames had burned themselves out. What happened to simmering flames?

He wasn't going to find out.

He went to the laundry nook off the kitchen and transferred the damp clothing to the dryer and turned it on. His jeans made a heavy thumping sound as they hit the drum and did battle with the more delicate clothing sharing the space.

"Do you mind if I pick this stuff up in the morning?" Livia was still asleep, and he hated to disturb her, but *he* needed some space. Needed to stop feeling his nerve endings thrumming.

Kat cocked her head. "Certainly. But…

it's raining. Do you want to wait until the worst is past? These are supposed to be quick squalls."

"I need to go."

"Why?"

"Because I don't want to."

Had he really just said that? Judging from the expression that had shot across Kat's face before she blanked it out, yes. Those words had come out of his mouth.

Do not blow things with the landlady.

He forced a smile. "What I mean is that I enjoy adult company, but I need to get Livia to bed—"

She put a hand on his chest, making both words and coherent thought skitter to a stop. He wasn't fooling her with talk of needing to get his daughter to bed. That was more than clear from the way she was looking at him. Maybe it was that look coupled with the fact that she'd forgotten to drop her hand from his chest. That had him stepping closer.

How long had it been since he'd kissed a woman?

However long it had been, the clock restarted a second later when he slid his hand under Kat's glorious hair to the back of her neck, gliding his fingers over soft, warm skin. She closed her eyes and rose on her toes to meet his lips. A quick taste, he told himself. A kiss between…landlord and tenant? Whatever.

Kat's free hand joined the one on his chest as the kiss deepened, and the quick taste became more of a starving man seeking sustenance. Kat lowered her heels to the ground, and it took Troy a moment to acknowledge the line he'd just crossed.

"That won't happen again."

He'd meant to be reassuring, but judging from the way Kat's expression shifted as she dropped her hands from his chest, he'd missed the mark.

"Don't read too much into this, Troy."

She spoke gently, but he felt the color rise in his cheeks. It wasn't that he was worried about himself. He was worried about sending the wrong message to Kat. Apparently, that needn't be a concern.

"Right." He reached up to squeeze the muscles at the back of his neck as Kat put some space between them. "It still won't happen again."

She raised her gaze toward the ceiling, tilting her head to listen. "It sounds like that rain has stopped. Guess you're free to go. I'm helping a friend tomorrow, but the house will be open, so you can get your laundry anytime."

THAT SELF-DISCIPLINE YOU'RE so proud of... What happened to it?

Kat punched her pillow and settled her head as the thought circled. She'd kissed the cowboy, or maybe he'd kissed her. Regardless of who started it, lips had connected, fireworks had ensued, and she had no idea what to make of it. But she'd liked it, and that worried her.

Kat rolled onto her back and stared up at the ceiling as she listened to the rain, which was finally slowing. Perhaps she didn't need to make anything of it, as long as she and Troy were on the same page. After they'd kissed, he'd looked like he wanted nothing more than to grab his baby and escape into the storm—which was exactly what he'd done—so she assumed they were in agreement.

Escape what though?

Her best guess was complications.

He had no worries there. She was also avoiding complications beyond the ones that she'd already signed on for, like making Littlegate Farm pay for itself. The new life she was building had room for one—herself.

That sounds super selfish, her little voice whispered.

So be it. Growing up, she'd taken on burdens no one asked her to shoulder. She'd been the self-assigned sheriff of the Farley family. Looking back, she could see that all she'd wanted was for her life to be free of surprises, because Farley surprises usually involved the potential for a ruined crop or a trip to the hospital.

She'd attempted to build a surprise-free life, complete with responsible boyfriend and secure career choices. Only she'd come to discover that there was no such thing as a surprise-free life, and that her responsible boyfriend was a manipulative rat.

Surprise.

Kat dropped an arm over her eyes.

She'd kissed the cowboy, but she was more concerned about the fact that she'd acted on impulse after assuring herself that she wouldn't. It had been too easy to convince herself that one little kiss wouldn't hurt.

It hadn't hurt. It'd felt really good.

Kissing Troy Mackay could lead to trouble, because if she lost control once, it could happen again.

CHAPTER FIVE

"You're going to trim my horses' hooves while your baby cries?" Patricia Knox, the owner of the five classy Arabians dancing around the small enclosure gave him an accusing look. In Troy's opinion, it was entirely unwarranted. Livia wasn't crying. Not even close. She was doing her presleep whimpers.

"She'll settle soon," he assured the woman.

He could tell that sleep wasn't far off, but Patricia Knox was having none of that. Her lips tightened as she announced, "I'll hold her."

"I'm sure she'll be—"

Patricia gave him a look, and he relented. "Thank you. And thank you for understanding why I brought her."

"That's not an issue with me. I raised

four kids. Life happens, and daycare often doesn't."

The way her face softened before she headed for the carrier told Troy that while he felt unprofessional, the woman didn't mind soothing his daughter. She'd probably keep Livia awake, and then he was going to be in for it with a cranky baby who didn't get her nap, but at the moment, he was more concerned with not losing a client.

That didn't appear to be a problem, though. Patricia patted Livia's back and closed her eyes as if recalling sweet memories of her own kids.

Troy led the first horse out of the enclosure and tied him to the outside railing. The gelding swung his butt around when Troy positioned him, and he patiently moved the horse back into position and picked up a front foot. The horse snatched it away and stamped it onto the ground. He chanced a glance at Patricia, but she was lost in baby land.

He pulled in a silent breath and continued the battle of wills with the gray gelding. Eventually, the horse gave up and allowed Troy to trim his feet. He paid special attention to the flare developing on the left front. Once the gelding was done, he released him into the next pen over and caught the sorrel mare.

"She doesn't like to be tied," Patricia said apologetically. "But she stands quietly once she knows you mean business."

"Right." Troy pulled his ball cap around backward.

Patricia held Livia the entire time that Troy trimmed her horses. She watched him as he worked with her skittish animals and seemed to approve of his technique.

"It's spring, and they need to burn off some energy," she said on a semi-apologetic note. "They were in a big pasture until last fall, but I lost the lease. I've had to make do with these little pens while I look for a place with more land." She looked at him over her glasses while lightly jiggling Livia against her shoulder. "Not easy right now."

"I know."

"But," she said as she regarded her animals, "these are my babies now that my others are grown. I'll figure something out."

By the time the last horse was done, Livia was conked out on Patricia's shoulder. Okay. No cranky baby.

"You did well," she said. "A lot of people get frustrated with them."

He couldn't imagine why, what with the horses yanking their feet out of his grip whenever they got the chance or sitting back on the rope. The horses were not held accountable by Patricia, that much was certain, but they were nice enough animals once they decided to settle. He was glad that all he was doing today was trimming, because he had a feeling that shoeing was going to be an adventure. As it was, he felt like he'd just run a half marathon.

Troy put his tools away as Patricia gently set the baby into her carrier. Livia made a protesting noise in her sleep but didn't wake.

"You're good with her," Troy said.

"I had practice." She gave Troy a look. "You can bring her anytime you want."

"I won't impose on you like that."

"My grandkids are hundreds of miles away on the other end of the state." She pulled out a wallet from her inside coat pocket. "Is cash okay?"

"If you insist." Troy gave her an amused look.

She smiled back before counting out the bills and handing them off to him. "You're off to Stenson's place next?"

"I am." He folded the cash, put it into his shirt pocket and snapped the flap. He'd lost money in the mud before and wasn't going to have it happen again. Not when he needed it so badly.

"Good luck with that gnarly beast." Patricia was serious. "Don't get hurt."

"I've handled my share of rank horses."

"I'm talking about Walt, not the stud."

Troy grinned and Patricia laughed. "But honestly? They're both cranky. Take care."

I'M SORRY I missed your dad," Kat said as she and Whitney rode out of the Fox Ranch corrals and headed across the pasture to the boundary fence they would check for breaks and stretched wire before turning out the cattle. She always enjoyed talking to Pete Fox. He ran his farm and ranching operations with the help of spreadsheets and computer programs. She often wondered what her family ranch would have been like if the planning had been a little less free-form. Granted, the Farley Ranch held its own thanks to her father's gut instincts, but a spreadsheet or two might have been beneficial.

"He left early this morning for the big fishing trip, but he said to tell you hello and that he's sure to bump into you now that you're back."

"He's not negotiating the riverbank with a cane, is he?"

"If he could do that, he'd be fixing fence with me. No. His friend bought a boat, and they're heading for the reservoir. If they're lucky, we'll have a fish fry tonight. If I'm lucky, we won't."

Kat laughed. "Taking off early tomorrow morning?"

"I am. I should still be able to get in full day's work if I stay late at the office." They rode across the field to the far gate, which

Whit opened from horseback. After Kat passed through, she closed it again.

"I always envied your gate abilities," Kat said with a smile. Gate opening from horseback was one of the more challenging obstacles in their 4-H trail-riding competition, and Whit had always made it look easier than it was.

"Like riding a bike." She adjusted the reins. "I envy you moving home." There was a note of wistful sincerity in her voice.

"You could, too, you know."

"Yes, but I'm kind of addicted to the steady paycheck, benefits and all that." She brushed her hair back. "And the nightlife in Missoula is fun."

"City girl," Kat murmured. Even though Missoula wasn't a sprawling metropolis, it was growing rapidly.

Whit gave her a stern look, which morphed into a grin. "We were such know-it-alls back then."

Back then being when Kat and Whit and Maddie had entered their freshman year of high school. They'd started dreaming about a future that wasn't as far away and unobtainable as it had seemed only a year before. They'd known they would soon be out in the world, making their own way and becoming massively successful in their chosen careers. Whit would train horses, Maddie would go to fashion school and design western wear, and Kat...

Kat had always planned to get her MBA. She'd wanted to move to a city and try out a different kind of life, one that didn't depend on the weather. Whit had teased her about becoming a city girl only to end up in a city herself. The horse training had not panned out, due to her winning a full-ride scholarship to an out-of-state university, an opportunity she couldn't pass up.

Of the three, Kat was the only one who'd followed the course of action set during their freshman year. She was still debating whether that was good or bad. Yes, she'd had a career independent of weather and fuel-price concerns, and she didn't need to worry about dreaded bovine diseases or the fickleness of the cattle and hay markets, but she'd never been able to shake the thought that her life was missing something.

She'd come to find out it was. She wasn't cut out to crunch numbers in an urban environment. She'd missed her rural roots, and she'd totally screwed up in the man department. One had little to do with the other, except that matters had come to a head simultaneously, thus linking them in her brain. Littlegate Farm was her way of breaking free. Now all she had to do was to hold on to the place.

Whit pulled her horse to a stop at the sagging barbwire fence. "I think this is where the mule deer cross."

"Looks like it." Kat dismounted and opened the saddle bag to pull out the hammer and box of staples.

"So…" Whit said, "have you held the baby yet?"

"Mr. Mackay is pretty protective of that baby."

"Swoon," Whit said with a grin.

If she hadn't felt like swooning a few times with said cowboy and baby, Kat might have laughed. Instead, she said, "He's…interesting."

And a great kisser. Straight up fact that

she couldn't avoid. What she did want to avoid was losing control again.

"Moving past your no-cowboy thing?" Whit asked.

Kat frowned. "I'm sure you're talking about having a cowboy as a friend."

"Of course that's what I meant," Whit said, all innocence.

"Good, because that's all I'm looking for, and I don't see that changing anytime soon."

"I understand." Whitney had never particularly liked Derek, and it showed in her voice.

Kat focused on the staple she was hammering. "Speaking of change, I swore I wouldn't change for anyone, and I did for Derek." It felt good to confess what her friend probably already knew. "I gave in too often, too easily. I'm kind of disgusted with myself."

"It was a frog-in-boiling-water thing," Whit said in a commiserative voice.

Kat was well familiar with the story of the poor amphibian being placed in slowly heated water so that it doesn't realize it's in trouble until it's too late. In general, she considered herself to be more self-aware than a frog, but that hadn't been the case with Derek. Slowly but surely, their relationship had drifted toward doing everything his way.

"Frog or not, it's sobering," she said.

"And a lesson learned," Whit said matter-of-factly.

"Oh yeah." Kat was not making that mistake again.

They moved on to the next post, leading the horses. Kat replaced another staple before attempting to lighten the mood by saying, "And I have to say that my no-cowboy thing made sense when you think about the cowboys we grew up with."

As in her brothers' wild friends.

"It did. Although you gotta admit, a lot of them were hot."

"Totally." Hot and unpredictable, the second characteristic trumping the first. Troy was hot and…predictable?

Yeah, he probably was now. She had a

feeling that back in the day, he'd been anything but.

"You know what?" Kat said as she positioned another staple over the wire. "Troy Mackay is my tenant. He doesn't need to be my friend."

"Where did that come from?" Whit asked with a curious look.

"If we're not friendly, I'll be less tempted to kiss him again."

"Wait. What?" Whit did a comical double take. "You kissed him?"

Kat gave a nonchalant shrug. "Maybe."

"Was it good?"

"It was."

"But you're not doing it again."

"I am not."

"You have more will power than I do," Whit said on a laugh, but Kat knew that her friend understood. Whit held her hand out for the staple box, and Kat handed it to her after taking one out. "But I get what you're saying. After Derek and all..."

Whit left the thought unfinished as she

focused on untangling two wires that were hooked together by the barbs.

Kat smacked a staple, and it bounced out of the wood, zinging toward Whit, who ducked. "Sorry."

Whit handed her another staple. "Expect the unexpected. Like kissing the tenant."

"But don't spend too much time worrying about it." Kat hit the staple squarely, and it sank into the wood. "That's my new motto."

That and don't kiss Troy Mackay.

WALT STENSON'S RANCH was an old run-down affair, but it was neat. The barn's roof sagged, but the area around it was raked. The corrals appeared sturdy but were made of weathered lodge poles that had probably been in place for at least fifty years. Three horses grazed in a grass pasture, and the stud he was about to shoe was in a pen three times the size of the ones that Patricia Knox kept her Arabians in.

As Troy pulled to a stop, a guy with a grizzled beard came out of the barn, waved and opened the gate to the stud's pen. Troy glanced in the back seat, assured himself that Livia was still asleep and went to meet the guy Patricia had described as a cranky old beast. Walt Stenson's first words gave him a hint as to why.

"How did you fare with Patricia's fancy-schmancy little horses?"

"No problems." Troy studied the big animal the man led into the stocks and tied. The stud was over sixteen hands with a thick mane and tail and a classic crested neck.

"Huh." Walt looked disappointed. Troy understood he was supposed to be the source of good gossip. When he'd apprenticed, he'd heard story after story about the inhabitants of the neighboring ranches from the farrier, because there wasn't much to do but gossip or tell tall tales while working on a horse's feet. It was a tedious business for those horse owners who chose to stay and watch, which most did. Farriers and salon personnel had their fingers on the pulse of the community.

As a newcomer, though, Troy was not

going to start his business by talking about other clients.

"I appreciate you coming today. I got some work this week, and I like to be here when a farrier works on Jack."

Jack let out a mighty snort at the sound of his name, and Livia let loose with a wail a split second later. Jack's ears shot forward at the sound. He snorted again and stamped a foot.

Excellent.

"What works with Jack?" Troy asked after checking the baby to make certain she was simply cranky and there was nothing else bothering her. She stopped crying when she saw her dad and then started again after he touched her cheek and headed back to horse and his impatient-looking owner.

Livia howled again, and the horse danced. Troy and Stenson exchanged looks, and as near as Troy could tell, Walt expected him to step up and start working on Jack's feet. Livia howled again. The horse snorted, and Troy's shoulders drooped.

"I apologize, Mr. Stenson. I can't do this today."

Stenson's mouth tightened into a grim line.

"I thought she would sleep."

"Doesn't appear to be the case," Stenson said. He shifted his weight. "Maybe if I hold her?"

Troy couldn't say he was wild about the idea of this man holding his daughter against his heavily stained barn coat with the patches of dried mud and who knew what. A crazy thought shot into his head.

"Would you be willing to push the stroller?"

The big man's bushy eyebrows lifted. "You have one of those with you?"

"I do." Like he'd go anywhere without it.

"You want me to push a stroller while you shoe Jack?"

"I'll give you a cut rate."

Stenson's lips pursed thoughtfully. "Sure."

Troy knew from Patricia, who had no qualms gossiping about people he didn't know, that most farriers charged Stenson extra to shoe his stud. They probably didn't bring babies with them.

Troy went back to the truck, pulled the stroller out of the back, where it rode next to his travel forge, and set it up. A moment later, he transferred Livia's car seat to the frame and snapped it into place.

Livia took a few hiccupping breaths and then launched another loud protest. Stenson approached the stroller cautiously and set a big hand on the handle.

"Do I do anything special?"

"Keep it moving, and she'll quiet." At least Troy hoped she would.

"If you say so." Stenson moved the stroller forward, and Livia stopped crying almost as soon as it started moving. "Wow."

"Yeah. Um...you might want to push her on the other side of the garage." He gestured toward Jack, who was eyeing the stroller like it was going to attack him.

"Right," Stenson said. "Good idea."

Troy turned his attention to the stud, who gave him the stink eye as Stenson and Livia disappeared behind the garage. "You and me, bud."

He got the nippers and the hoof knife out of his shoeing box, turned his ball cap around backward and headed toward the stud. In the distance, he could hear stroller wheels fighting gravel, but Livia wasn't crying. He wasn't going to allow himself to think about what this was going to do to his professional reputation, but he knew for a fact that he was not taking any more jobs when he had to bring his kid. Not even last-minute ones as a favor.

In the end, Troy won the battle of wills with Jack, but not before he'd gotten knocked sideways, nearly stepped on and had dodged a ferocious bite aimed at the back of his thigh. It was obvious why farriers charged more for Jack, but true to his word, he cut the price for Stenson.

"Will you be back?" the man asked. He was clearly used to farriers cutting and running after a session or two with Jack.

"Yes, but in the future, I have to work around daycare."

"Pushing the stroller wasn't that bad."

And neither was paying half rate to get his cranky stud's feet done, Troy guessed.

"I won't be bringing any little apprentices next time."

"Suit yourself," Stenson said, untying his horse. "Like I said. It wasn't that bad."

LIVIA SLEPT ALL the way home after their shoeing adventure, waking as Troy drove over the cattle guard at the entrance to Littlegate Farm. Instead of complaining, she cooed a couple of times. He glanced into the rearview mirror and could see her little hands waving about.

He'd had a successful day, all things considered, and there was money in his pocket, although not as much as he would have had if he hadn't given Stenson a cut rate. One thing was certain. He needed steady daycare. He would not be bringing his daughter out on jobs unless it was a flat-out emergency. It was too stressful, and he hated feeling unprofessional.

How would he feel if he hired a plumber who showed up with a baby? He had to admit that if he desperately needed a plumber, he probably wouldn't care. He might even hold the baby, but that didn't change the fact that he needed to work around childcare.

He kicked himself for not giving baby-sitting more thought before he'd moved to Larkspur. He'd been in an excellent situation while working for Michaels' Short Haul. Grace had watched Livia while he drove, often bringing her to the office. She'd taught Troy a lot of parenting tricks in the process, so he'd had no idea about the reality of professional daycare. He'd foolishly figured that daycares would accept drop-ins and that he could pop Livia in and out at will. *Yeah.* He should have done some research instead of making assumptions.

"We'll plan better next time," he said to Livia as he pulled up next to the tree beside his trailer. Kat's car was gone, so he and Livia had the ranch to themselves. After feeding and changing her, he scooped her up and headed out the door to stretch his legs. He appreciated the trailer, but it was small, and he was not the kind of guy who enjoyed being cooped up. Much better to look for a project that would allow him to work off part of the debt he owed Kat.

He was doing a survey of the corrals near the barn, which obviously hadn't seen inhabitants for a number of years, when he heard the sound of an engine. Thinking it was Kat, he came around the barn in time to see a fancy Range Rover pull to a stop on the opposite side of the cattle guard.

Troy shifted Livia and raised a hand in a friendly wave, thinking it was a friend of Kat's who didn't know she was renting to him. Instead of driving onto the farm, the car reversed and backed onto the county road.

Lost tourist perhaps? The Rover had Montana plates.

The driver appeared to change his or her mind, then. The windows were tinted to the point that it was hard to tell anything about the occupants of the car at this distance. Instead of completing the turn onto county road, the driver once again pulled into the farm drive.

The Rover stopped a few yards from Troy, who hefted Livia a little higher in his arms before approaching the rig. A blond guy in his thirties got out, flashing a smile at Troy as he closed the door.

"Hi. I'm looking for Kat Farley."

The sign on the side of the Rover read, Cashman Properties, which Troy took to mean real estate. Was this the guy who'd brokered the deal between Kat and her aunt? If so, he might know of rentals in the area.

"She's helping a friend right now. It may take all day."

"Ah." The blond glanced down at the gravel between them and then back up at Troy. He clearly was curious as to who Troy was, but as they continued their silent face-off, Troy realized there was something about the guy that made him not want to volunteer information. Strange how a person could rub you the wrong way simply by the way he carried himself.

"Are you a friend?" Troy asked, sensing that this guy with the important attitude wouldn't want to be the first one questioned.

"Are you?"

Troy smiled. "Business associate." If this guy turned out to be a friend of Kat's, he'd come clean later. Right now, he chose to tread lightly.

"Yeah?" The guy hadn't reacted, but Troy got the impression that he didn't like what he'd just heard. "What business is that?"

"Property."

Now there was a reaction—slight but readable. No. Troy didn't like the vibe of the man.

"Can I tell Kat who stopped by?"

The blond man's gaze cut to the sign on his vehicle, as if realizing there was no sense in saying no. "Yes." The professional smile was back, but he wasn't happy. "Tell her that Dane Cashman stopped to see her. I have a business proposition that would benefit us *both*." He emphasized the last word. "All I ask is that she hear me out."

"Is there a reason she wouldn't?" Troy asked in a reasonable tone.

"She and my brother dated until recently, but I guess as her business associate, you would know that. I don't want the past to interfere with what could be a very bright future for both of us."

Troy gave a slow nod. He hadn't liked this guy before, and he liked him even less now. "I'll tell her."

Dane Cashman stood for a moment, as if waiting for more—although Troy had no idea what. A ring kiss, maybe?—then he gave Troy a tight smile. "Thanks. I appreciate it." He nodded at Livia, who was peeking at him from Troy's shoulder. "Cute kid."

Troy didn't bother answering, and a few seconds later, Dane Cashman was back in his vehicle, all but invisible behind the tinted windows. The Rover executed a three-point turn and bumped over the cattle guard before Troy moved.

"I don't like him, Button." He rubbed a hand over the back of his daughter's pink flowered shirt as she let go of his ear and laid her head on his shoulder. He would give Kat the message. Maybe he'd read the guy wrong. Maybe he really was a friend, and the strange vibe came from the fact that his brother had dated Kat. He had to admit he was curious to see what her reaction would be.

One thing was certain, though. He would not be asking Dane Cashman about potential rentals in the area.

CHAPTER SIX

TROY WAITED FOR a little over hour after Kat's return before heading across the driveway. She called for him to come in when he knocked on her screen door, and he found her unpacking boxes in her kitchen.

"I hate moving," she said. "I'm going to try to keep from doing it again."

"This is your forever home then?"

"Yes." Kat set a stack of nesting mixing bowls on the table and pushed her hair back. "I've lost a small sock."

"Let's check the dryer."

They did, and Troy found the little fuzzy sock adhered to the drum. He tucked it into his shirt pocket. "This is my life now. The search for small socks."

"This is my life for a while," she said, nodding at the boxes.

"You had a visitor today."

Kat shot him a curious look.

"Dane—" The expression that transformed her face upon hearing the single name brought him to a stop. No further identification necessary.

"Really?" She shot an aggravated look at the ceiling.

"Yeah. He had a message."

"I'm sure he did." She cocked her head.

"He said he'd like you to hear him out on a business deal that would benefit both of you."

"That's not going to happen."

Kat's clipped tone told Troy that he was justified in not liking Dane Cashman. "Is this guy going to be trouble?"

She dove back into the box and came up with some cake pans. She set them next to the mixing bowls and leaned back against the counter. "Nothing I can't handle. More of an annoyance, really."

Like being a reminder of a guy she used to date?

"Okay. Well, I've got my sock, so…"

She folded her arms over her chest, her hip still resting against the counter. "You remember yesterday? When you said you didn't want to go?"

The moment was pretty much etched into his brain.

"I recall the aftermath... Not that I'm reading too much into it." He echoed the words she'd spoken after the kiss.

"I shouldn't have kissed you."

"It was mutual," he stated. "And we're good."

She pushed back her curls, and Livia nearly toppled out of Troy's arms as she reached out to bat at Kat's hair. He captured his daughter's hand before she could grab hold and pull, which was one of her favorite moves and the reason he kept his own hair short. Kat gave his little girl a quick smile and moved back a step.

"I told myself the easiest way to handle this would be to put some distance between us." Kat's mouth twisted ruefully. "To back off and stop being friendly, but that's not how I want to live. Not on my own property." She once again folded her arms over her middle as she studied the floor between them. "That said, my life is *not* very orderly at the moment, and I'm not looking for more complications."

"Sometimes life smacks you, and you have to step back and assess."

She met his eyes, and he felt a jolt of connection that didn't jibe with the words he was saying. He pushed the feeling aside.

"Yes," she said softly. "There's nothing like a good smack to keep one aware of potential consequences."

THE FACT THAT Dane Cashman had made a special trip to her farm bothered Kat, despite her determination to ignore the man. Knowing his game might be an advantage, but she couldn't think of anything he could do to change her situation, no matter how badly he might want to cut some kind of a deal on the farm. And what kind of deal did he have in mind? A lease? A purchase? Joint venture?

As if she would enter into any kind of business dealings with the brother of the man that had tried to gaslight her. He might want her farm, for reasons unknown, but it wasn't like he could do anything about it. The deal was done, and the sour grapes were his to deal with alone.

At least that's what she thought until she entered the offices of OPM—O'Brien Property Management—for her scheduled appointment to discuss the company's bookkeeping needs.

Ada Mason, the OPM office manager and a friend of Kat's mother, blinked when Kat walked through the door. She was obviously surprised to see her.

"Hi, Kat." There was an overly bright note to her voice that set free butterflies in Kat's stomach. "What can I do for you?"

Kat worked up a smile, hoping that Ada had just forgotten she was on their calendar.

"I have an appointment with Mr. O'Brien."

"Oh, I'm sorry." Ada dropped her hands into her lap. "I thought Mary had called you."

"About...?"

Ada's face took on an apologetic expression. "I'm afraid we will not be needing your services."

"Temporarily?"

"We've done some restructuring. Mr. O'Brien had planned on using contract accountants, but we've decided to go with a firm. We're expanding, and well…"

"I see."

She didn't. She'd sent out a blanket email to all the business in Larkspur, advertising her services while she was in the process of buying Littlegate Farm, and Dennis O'Brien had responded enthusiastically, setting up the appointment that Mary had neglected to cancel.

Ada looked like she wanted to give Kat a hug instead of more bad news. "I'm sorry, Kat."

"I… I'm surprised," she finally said. She wasn't about to kill the messenger, but she'd like the messenger to give her more information if possible.

"Mary should have called."

"A restructuring."

"Yes."

Ada cut her gaze sideways in a way that caught Kat's attention and pursed her lips as if trying to keep from speaking. Finally, after a quick glance toward Dennis

O'Brien's closed office door, the woman met Kat's gaze. "You didn't hear this from me."

Kat's stomach felt like it had compressed to the size of a walnut. "You're my mom's friend. Of course I wouldn't say anything."

"You ruffled the feathers of a fellow business owner. One that Dennis works closely with at times. That's all I know."

Kat gave a slow nod. "Thank you, Ada."

"Take care, Kat."

Kat didn't know if the woman was saying goodbye or giving her a warning. She managed a smile of sorts. "Well, you never know. Things might work out later."

"Yes. They very well might."

Kat left the office and then stood for a moment outside the door, debating next moves. The morning sun was warm, and the air was clear after the cleansing rain the night before. It was a beautiful day, but Kat barely registered.

Do battle or go home?

She glanced at the offices of Cashman Properties directly across the street. She had no illusions as to whose feathers she'd ruffled, although she thought of Dane Cashman as being scaled rather than feathered.

Cashman Properties was a real estate outfit. OPM managed properties for wealthy clients, taking care of places for absentee owners, which Montana had its fair share of thanks to blisteringly cold winters that many people chose not to endure. She could see where Dennis O'Brien and Dane Cashman might have a symbiotic relationship, and that had given Dane the clout to poison her potential professional relationship with OPM.

She jaywalked across the nearly empty street, jogging at the last minute to avoid an ancient pickup truck that came barreling around the corner onto Main. By the time she reached Dane's office, her heart was pounding, and it wasn't from exertion, nor was it from fear of confrontation. It was anger that had her heart thumping harder, and she was itching to take it out on someone—that someone being a well-groomed rat hiding behind an office door.

Like Ada, Dane's associate appeared

startled by Kat suddenly striding into the tasteful offices of Cashman Properties. The woman was young and perfectly attired in a tailored blue dress with a simple gold chain. Her blond hair was pulled back into a tasteful chignon.

"I want to see Dane," Kat said. There would be none of this "Mr. Cashman" bull.

"I'm sorry—" The associate jumped to her feet in response to Kat walking past her desk to pound on the oak door of Dane's lair. It opened before her hand touched wood.

"I'm sorry, Mr. Cashman. I—"

Dane waved aside the explanation. "That's all right. I'll see Miss Farley."

Kat merely tipped her chin when he made an ushering gesture into his office. "We can talk here." She had no problem having a witness to what she was going to say.

Dane's lips tightened. He nodded at Miss Farley, who dipped her chin close to her chest as she passed by on her way to the back rooms. When the door had closed behind her, Dane said, "You certainly were quick to replace my brother." There was no malice in his voice. He spoke as if citing a curious fact.

"He's not a replacement," she said. "Replacement implies similar characteristics. I wouldn't have another man like your brother in my life." She was pretty certain she wasn't going to have another man in her life period.

"So this guy is...different?"

"This guy is my tenant."

"Ah," he said as if suddenly understanding something that he'd been wondering about.

"I'm not interested in selling the farm, Dane. I'm not changing my mind, so you should find another property to pursue."

"You Farleys." He spoke with what sounded like affectional amusement. Or maybe it was poorly disguised condescension.

Really?

Kat kept her expression mildly curious as she folded her arms over her chest. "What about us?"

"You dive in over your head without a

thought to what might happen. I have to say, you seemed different to me."

"Guess not."

"I understand the emotions involved in your decision to keep Margo's property in the family, and how that might have led to hasty action."

"Without regarding consequences?" she asked. Because her brothers were pretty famous for that.

"Some consequences take time rearing their heads. A person might not initially be aware they exist."

"Really?" She'd stormed across the street to explain to Dane that if he messed with her livelihood again, he would regret it. But she could see that was exactly what he wanted. He wanted her upset. He wanted to get to her.

"I'm not interested in selling," she said again. "But if I were…" She drew the last word out. "What is this business opportunity that would benefit both of us?" Because if she was going up against this guy, she wanted all the ammo she could get, and understanding his motivations would help immensely.

Dane's eyes lit up, and he shifted gears into smooth salesmanship. "Here's the thing, Kat. Littlegate Farm is a money pit. We both know that. The buildings need roofs. The house needs to be redone inside and out. The property fences are a menace. Yes, you get to live on the land your aunt loved, but what good is that if it slowly slips away? The capital involved in putting the place right will be substantial."

"Yet you're interested in the property."

"Before it deteriorates more. It's salable now, but the price will go down as more things fall apart."

She smiled a little. "Your concern is commendable considering the fact that your brother and I had a rather bad ending to our relationship, thanks to his duplicity."

"I'm a businessman, Kat. I'm sorry you and Derek had issues, but that has nothing to do with what I'm proposing. I'd love to earn the commission on your place, and if you put it up for sale, I could get you more than you paid Margo. You would make a profit. I would make a profit. Then you could buy something with a lot more potential, even if it doesn't hold the sentimental value of Littlegate Farm."

"Which you would sell to me?"

"Owner pays the commission. It would cost you nothing, and I have some sweet properties that would be perfect for you to start a little horse ranch or whatever suits your fancy."

"Why do you really want my place, Dane?

His smile didn't waver. "I told you. I'm a businessman."

That might be true, but it didn't explain why he'd been so interested in the place prior to her breakup with his brother. Why he'd gone so far as to intercede on her dealings with Dennis O'Brien, thus affecting her income.

"It's definitely a fixer-upper," she said. "I don't see it getting top dollar unless you plan to subdivide."

Dane's face remained impassive. She might have hit the nail on the head, but she didn't see how. Littlegate Farm was isolated, and while Larkspur was charming, it was far enough away from big shops that it hadn't experienced the growth of some other Montana towns. But still...

"Is that it, Dane? You want to subdivide?"

"I told you what I want. I'd try to get the best deal for both of us. You would walk away a winner, and think how much better your life would be on a property that isn't so run-down. You'd still be close to family and more able to focus on your business."

The emphasis on the last word was so subtle that had she not just come from Dennis O'Brien's, she might have thought she'd imagined it. It made her spine stiffen.

"So you had a word with Dennis O'Brien."

"About what?" There was just enough smugness in his expression to confirm her suspicions. He'd talked Mr. O'Brien out of using her services.

Kat narrowed her eyes at the man who looked so much like her ex it kind of creeped her out. Dane stared back as if daring her to accuse him of something. Why bother? He knew that she knew, and hearing his denial of any involvement in her affairs would only serve to aggravate her.

"Let me explain something to you, Dane. You aren't getting my farm. Stop trying." She turned on her heel and strode to the door. Before she pushed it open, she abruptly stopped to look back at the man, who was still standing on the opposite side of his associate's desk. "Don't screw with my business again, or I'll have you in court."

"Where I believe you have the burden of proof, and the last I heard, it's hard to prove a fantasy."

Kat lifted her lips into a confident half-smile. "Try me, Dane. Try me and see what happens."

AFTER KAT LEFT for her meeting in town, Troy spent Livia's nap time tarring the shingles on the roof, breaking his own rule about climbing ladders when alone. He'd left the door to the trailer open to hear Livia if she cried, and he had just finished cleaning up when he heard her announce that she was awake and ready for company and a meal.

After finishing Dad duties, he settled Livia against his shoulder and headed to the corrals to inventory what he was going to need there for repairs. He tapped a list into his phone with the thumb of one hand while securing Livia with the other. When the weather got nicer, he'd spread a blanket on the grass near the corral, and she could play there while he worked.

Or she could tune up and cry as she was getting ready to do now.

Troy made a silly face at Livia as the corners of her mouth turned down. Sometimes, he could charm her out of crying, but not today. The wailing began, and Troy started bouncing her with one arm as he continued the inventory, making mental notations instead of typing them into a list.

It became apparent that Livia wasn't going to be soothed by bouncing, so Troy gave up the task and headed to the trailer to see about food and diapers, even though he'd already covered those bases. Something was up, and he wasn't going to be able to get anything done until he figured out how to make his little girl feel better. Sometimes, she simply got so caught up in crying that she couldn't stop, and this was starting to feel like one of those times.

He'd just gotten to the trailer when his phone rang.

"Are you the shoer who did Patricia Knox's horses?"

Livia let out a scream that made Troy grimace. He wondered if the lady on the other end of the line was doing the same.

"I am. Sorry about that."

"Would you be available to reset some shoes? One mare. Good with her feet."

The jobs were coming, and he didn't know if he would be able to take them. Troy swallowed his frustration and laid Livia in her bassinet. She let out a cry that made him want to scoop her back up again. Instead, he silently promised her that he'd be right back and stepped outside the trailer, closing the door to muffle the crying.

"Hi again. Sorry about that. I would be happy to reset shoes, but I won't be able to do it until next Thursday." When he'd booked Livia's first official drop-in day at Daisy Lane Daycare, hoping he'd be able to book jobs that day.

"Could you squeeze me in before Friday?"

"Of this week?"

"I have an event. My farrier baled on me."

"I... Let me call you back?"

"Sure, but I'm going to have to continue to look for someone."

"Understood. Thank you. I'll get back to you as soon as I can."

The call ended before he got the last word out. Troy lowered the phone and ran a hand over the back of his neck.

Right.

He headed back into the trailer and lifted a red-faced Livia out of the bassinet. She laid her head against his shoulder and continued to sob.

"I understand," he said as he rubbed her back. He didn't, really, but it seemed like the thing to say.

He'd known going in that single parenthood was going to have challenges. He was butting up against one now, but, unlike his parents, when things got challenging, he didn't have, nor did he want, the option of throwing money at it. He was simply going to have to get used to the idea of giving up jobs on the days that he couldn't finagle childcare.

This is temporary, he reminded himself as he bounced his crying daughter. Someday she'd be all about not needing him, but right now, she did. He wasn't going to let her down.

He paced the floor until Livia gave a hiccup followed by a burp, making him think that gas had been the culprit and the trouble might be over. Indeed, her little body relaxed after the burp, so Troy settled her into her carrier, where she started reaching for the toys hanging from the handle, an expression of extreme concentration on her face as she attempted to grab the fox's fuzzy tail.

"Atta girl, Button," Troy said as she got the tail and pulled it close enough to get it into her mouth.

His phone rang as Livia let go of the fox's tail and tried for the flamingo.

Maybe the potential client he'd just spoken was calling to say she'd found someone else?

No. Not a lost job.

"Sass." He smiled as he said his former travel partner's name. Saskia Belmont was something of a barrel racing legend. They'd met on a blind date early in Troy's career but had both agreed they shared no physical chemistry. They'd liked one another tremendously, though.

Soon thereafter, they'd become travel buddies and mutual sounding boards, living separate lives when they weren't sharing a truck but still keeping in contact.

Sass was also an only kid, although her parents had doted on her, and Troy found himself thinking of her as the sister he'd never had. As such, if he needed advice, he asked. If he had advice, he offered.

Sass had been the one to gently ask him if he thought Tiff was the right woman for him less a month before their impulsive Vegas wedding. The question had surprised him. Tiff was funny, charming, caring, had a ton of self-confidence and essentially lit up any room she walked into.

He'd had no idea he was dating a narcissist. He'd done his research too late, after he'd come to realize that for all of her charm, Tiff wasn't going to make the same sacrifices for him that he would make for her. And there definitely would be no children. He'd told himself he could accept that. And he had. Now he knew he was meant to be a dad. Oddly, he no longer harbored hard feelings toward Tiff. She'd been honest about her abilities. He'd been the one who'd made assumptions.

That didn't mean his world hadn't been ripped apart when they'd bowed to the reality of their incompatibility and called it quits. He'd always been a winner, and then he wasn't.

He wasn't going to test relationship waters again until he was at a point where it wouldn't affect his daughter.

"How's the new job?" he asked. Sass had gone to work for a private rodeo touring company last fall, shortly after he'd quit rodeo and gone to work for Michaels Short Haul Trucking.

"I love it. How's the kid?"

"Growing."

"I bet. Hey… I'm calling with an offer."

"What kind of offer," Troy asked slowly.

"You know the tour we're putting on this fall. The Unrideable?"

"I do." Because she'd kept him updated on it.

"I lost a participant. I need another. Interested?"

He felt a jolt of adrenaline at the thought of going on tour, then reality came crashing in. "I have a job nailed down here, Sass. Full time. Benefits. All the grown-up stuff I've been avoiding."

"It's a special tour, Troy. It's an honor to be invited."

"I don't want to raise Livia on the road."

"One tour is not the same as raising your kid on the road."

He was out of shape, but he wasn't going to mention that.

"I'll babysit, Troy."

"I don't know if you've got what it takes."

"I'll learn. This is a good opportunity. You can rebuild that nest egg. We can drive together. It'll be like old times."

"Plus one."

"She's small. Won't take up much room."

Saskia was unaware of the size of the car seat.

"Sass, it hurts me to say no, but I have to go with the full-time job. Benefits. All that."

She didn't answer immediately, and when she did, he could hear the disappointment in her voice. "Think about it. I'll call again in a few days."

"Sass, I've gotta say no. Sorry."

"I understand." He heard her pull in a breath before adding, "But if you change your mind, call me. No guarantees, but if there's an opening, it's yours."

He glanced at his daughter, the reason he was choosing the responsible path, and her little face crumpled as their gazes met.

"I'll call next week," she said.

"Great. But do it to catch up."

"Or to wear you down. No promises as to which it'll be."

He smiled a little. "Right."

Livia let out a mighty cry before the call ended, to which Sass said, "Wow. Lungs. I'll be in touch, Troy Boy."

"Looking forward to it." He ended the call and gently lifted his daughter from the carrier. She was a clinger today, and something was obviously bothering her.

Normal kid stuff or something more?

He wished Grace was here to advise him. She'd helped him navigate the unknowns of early infancy, and he honestly didn't know what he'd have done without her. After a run of bad luck, he'd been blessed with a boss who was also a grandmother and who loved looking after his tiny daughter while he drove. He'd tried to pay her, but she'd have none of it.

Now he was navigating these waters alone, and it was mildly terrifying.

CHAPTER SEVEN

SWEAT TRICKLED BETWEEN Kat's shoulder blades as she put aside the digger and eased the post into the hole she'd just dug. Bringing the fences up to standard was no small task after at least a decade of Montana winters wreaking havoc on posts and wire with no one doing regular maintenance and repairs. Now she had to undo the damage.

Dane Cashman's attempt to do her financial harm had partially backfired, because two days after their face-off, Ada Mason with O'Brien Property Management contacted Kat to say that they had a client looking for a place to keep their horses while their facilities were being built. They needed someone to accommodate two Tennessee walkers in two weeks' time.

Kat was certain she could. It was a small consolation for losing what could have been a lucrative contract with a local business, but it could help kick-start her horse-boarding business.

She'd yet to fully inspect her fences when she'd made the promise, and upon doing so, she'd realized that she had a serious job on her hands.

If there was one thing Kat was a master of, besides numbers, it was fencing. She'd repaired miles of the stuff on the family ranch, and if her brothers hadn't all been fully booked, she would have enlisted their help. However, all three had their hands full either working for the home ranch or contracting their services to surrounding farms and ranches that were shorthanded. Kat wasn't going to add to their workload when she was perfectly capable of handling the fencing alone. If she got desperate, she'd ask Troy for help, but so far, so good.

Would you really ask? And then spend the day in close contact with a guy who makes your nerves hum?

Rather than answer herself, Kat started kicking dirt into the hole, holding the post upright as she did so. She calculated that she'd be able to get the fences fixed and new feeders in place before her potential clients came to inspect the facilities next week, but she was also going to have to work into the night to keep up with her bookkeeping obligations.

She didn't mind. For the first time in years, she felt right, like she was living the life she was meant to live, instead of trying to force herself into a life that didn't quite fit. Whit's sweater analogy was so spot-on. She hadn't been comfortable, but she'd been warm, and she'd told herself that was enough.

It was not, and now that she'd found a life she wanted, she was not going to let anything, or anyone, screw things up. And that included her tenant—not that he would mess things up on purpose. That would be totally on her. He was respectful and private and spending too much time in her head. Maybe because in regard to openness and honesty, he was the opposite of Derek—or appeared to be.

That was the kicker. She didn't know. She'd thought Derek was a good guy—and he did have good qualities, as most people do—but she let the things she liked about him and the security of having a responsible partner keep her from acknowledging the little red flags that had cropped up every now and again. She should have paid closer attention. Lesson learned, and once Kat learned a lesson, she did not forget.

Kat tamped the dirt around the base of the post and used a level to make certain it wasn't leaning in one direction or another before kicking in more dirt and tamping again. When the fencepost was firmly set, she loaded her tools in the back of the truck and surveyed her progress—a good half mile of tightened fence with three rotten posts replaced. A decent day's work, soon to be followed by a decent night's work at her computer.

She did not mind the long hours now that she was her own boss. She had a farm that she loved and—most importantly—no one was messing with her emotions. Three times blessed, and she was going to work her butt off to keep things that way.

Kat pulled in a deep breath of fresh Montana air and took a moment to admire the beauty of the quiet pasture bordered by the stand of timber that separated Littlegate Farm from the Bealman property next door.

This was all hers. Eighty acres of pasture and potential. All she had to do was get the fences repaired and work on the feeders—

The thought stuttered to a halt as she turned and caught sight of a thin plume rising from the direction of her house and barn.

A plume that looked a lot like smoke.

She jerked open the door and scrambled into the truck, turning on the ignition before shutting the door. The last thing she needed was to watch her dream farm go up in smoke.

TROY SAW THE smoke when he started down the long driveway leading from Kat's mailbox to Littlegate Farm. Not a lot of smoke, but enough to make him wonder what Kat was burning. Brush? A ditch? It was late in the season for that, and unless she'd just started, there wasn't enough smoke for that kind of a burn.

He hit the gas, and when he emerged from the stand of fir at the cattle guard, the source of the smoke was obvious—a small building near the old grain silo was engulfed in flames. He vaulted out of his truck, noting that there were electrical wires going to the burning shed. Where was the breaker box? House, garage, barn?

He was almost to the barn when Kat's truck came bouncing across the pasture. She jumped out at the gate and raced toward him.

"Where's the breaker box?"

"Barn."

"Go flip the main power switch. Do you know—"

"I know." She dashed into the barn while he gathered the hose beneath the standpipe and connected it to the faucet.

"Everything is off," she called, and Troy started the water.

The building was small—outhouse size, which he suspected had been its original purpose—and the standpipe had good water pressure, so it didn't take long to put out the flames. Troy kept the water running long after the last flicker of orange disappeared beneath the spray.

"I think you have it," Kat finally said from beside him. She went forward to inspect what was left of the structure— a few charred uprights and ashes—then shook her head. "I had to have an electrical inspection on the house to qualify for my mortgage," she said. "You would have thought they'd have also inspected the outbuildings, but maybe not."

"Maybe it wasn't electrical," Troy said, earning himself a sharp look.

"What do you mean?"

The color that had been coming back into her cheeks seemed to drain away again.

"My point is that maybe you should get a fire marshal, or whoever looks at these things, out here to make sure."

"What other cause could there be?" she asked. "It isn't like there's anything there to spontaneously combust."

"Why is an outhouse wired for electricity?"

"Maybe someone wanted to read." Kat shook her head as she regarded the charred remains of the small building. "It has to be an accident," she said more to herself than to him. "And that means electrical." She turned to Troy. "You're right. I'm going to get an electrician to check things out as soon as possible."

"Probably a good idea." He wanted to know why she had any question about it being an accident. He didn't want to push his nose into matters that were not his concern, but while he was living here with his baby daughter, it was his concern.

"Look at the condition of the wiring," he said. The wire laying on the ground near them was partially burned, but it was also worn where it wasn't burned, and… Was that electrical tape covering a bare spot?

"Yes. I haven't had time to take a close look at everything on the place, but this needs looked at now." She muttered something about counting on inspectors to catch this kind of thing as she pulled out her phone. A moment later, she said, "James, I need Squeak's number. The old outhouse caught fire— No. No one was in it." She rolled her eyes. "It looks like wiring, and no, I don't know why an outhouse was wired. I want a quick once-over of the rest of the wiring so that I can sleep." She smiled grimly and shot Troy a quick look. He lifted an eyebrow in response. "Just a sec…" She started punching buttons into her phone. "Thanks, and everything is under control. Troy is here, so…yes. I have this. No rescue. Got it?"

She let out a breath as she ended the call. "I hate feeling like I'm the youngest instead of the oldest."

"Brothers can be protective," Troy said.

She glanced up from her phone. "Do you have a sister?"

"My parents barely survived me." *My parents barely acknowledged me* would be more accurate, but Troy shook off the thought and continued, "I've known some protective brothers in my day."

"Were you dating their sisters?"

"Maybe." He grinned and was glad to see Kat smile in return. Having a fire on the property was serious business, but it was out, and she was calling in an expert, so all was well—or as well as it could be.

Kat turned her attention to the phone and punched the button for the number James had given her. "Squeak, it's Kat Farley."

She explained what had happened, and to Troy's surprise, it sounded like Squeak would be over in an hour. "Thanks, Squeak."

"An hour?"

"We go way back," she explained as she ended the call. "Sport teams, homerooms. That kind of stuff."

"I'm looking forward to meeting an electrician named Squeak. It's a better name than Sparky."

"Her name is Amy Greensboro. We called her Squeak because she had the unique ability to squeak out of dicey situations without getting in trouble, unlike the rest of us."

"Us?"

"I didn't get into a lot of trouble," she admitted. "But I wasn't a wuss, either. The thing is, most of my energies were directed toward keeping my brothers *out* of trouble and helping them cover their tracks when they did something dumb. Aiding and abetting when I couldn't prevent."

"Big sister stuff?"

"Which is why they have no business trying to rescue me," she muttered. She met his gaze. "I like doing things my own way. Handling my own situations."

He lifted his hands. "I won't interfere."

She directed her gaze back to the remains of the outhouse. The ashes were wet, but wisps of smoke were showing here and there.

"Livia is still asleep in the truck, so I'll water this down some more."

She gave him a long look. "Thank you."

He had a feeling that she had something else to say—maybe something along the lines of she'd take care of since she'd just made a point about preferring to handle things by herself.

Instead, she said, "You won't have power in the trailer until Squeak gives the all-clear."

"I've dry-camped before."

"With a baby?"

"No."

She considered for a moment. "Feel free to use my kitchen and bathroom." Her house being on a separate electrical system might explain why the outbuilding wiring apparently hadn't been inspected prior to her qualifying for the mortgage.

"I will."

"I mean it."

He couldn't help but smile at her accurate read of his intention to only use her house if absolutely necessary. "I will," he repeated. "A baby needs water."

"So do grown men."

"There are times." He held up the hose he was using to spray the ashes.

"Touché." She might be smiling, but the fire had shaken her, as well it should. Buying a farm and starting a new life shouldn't involve flames.

"I'm sure this was a fluke," he said.

Livia let out a loud wail before Kat could answer, and she held out her hand for the hose.

"I'll handle this. You better see about your baby."

"Right." He wanted to tell her that everything would be okay, that he had her back. One look at her rapidly closing expression told him not to bother. She wanted to handle things alone, and she would, regardless of whether he had her back or not.

LIVIA WAS HAVING a night, crying inconsolably, which meant that Troy was also having a night.

As was Kat, who put a hand over her forehead as the sound of Livia's distress wafted in through the open bedroom window.

The fire had rattled her concentration. She tried to focus on data entry as she caught up on her day job—which she did at night—but her mind kept drifting back to the fire and to how glad she'd been to have Troy there to help deal with it.

Once she reached that point in her mental rehash, she had to convince herself that she was not sliding toward dependency. It bothered her that Troy had kind of taken over, and it bothered her more that she'd let him. But it wasn't like she could have said everything was fine and he should go about his business while she deal with the fire.

There had to be a middle ground.

Squeak, who looked the same as she had in high school, with a bouncy blond pony-tail and a mischievous smile, had shown up less than an hour after Kat's call. After inspecting the burn, she agreed that the cause of the fire was probably old, weathered wiring, and then she had meticulously checked the wiring and junctions in the house and outbuildings, even risking an owl attack to inspect the attic.

"You have three owlets up there," she said when she came back down through the trapdoor unscathed. "Hungry owlets. But they're not eating the wiring. Everything looks good. I checked Dad's records, and he upgraded the house in 1991. I hate to think what it might have been like before then, given the age of the place."

"So not much risk of another electrical fire."

"I'd say you're in good shape. Except for that outhouse. Why it was wired…"

"Actually, I know." Her mother had filled her in when she'd called to make certain that her only daughter was all right. "It was for a heater in the winter. Now I remember my aunt laughing about it when I was a kid. They couldn't afford to add a bathroom onto the house in the 1940s, so they invested in a heater for the outhouse. Thankfully, by the time I stayed with my aunt, they had indoor plumbing."

Squeak shuddered. "I hate it when I have to get up during the night. I can only imagine getting up and traveling through the cold and dark."

"We're spoiled," Kat agreed. She paid Squeak and walked with her to her utility truck.

"You're back for good?" Squeak asked.

"I am," Kat said. It felt good saying the words with conviction. "It's good to come home."

"Going to give yourself an ulcer trying to keep up with your brothers?"

"Nope. I'm going to give them an ulcer trying to keep up with me."

Squeak laughed. "Turnabout. Love it."

At nine o'clock, after she'd finally focused enough to finish data entry, Kat turned off her computer and stretched. It was too early for bed, and it wasn't like she was going to fall asleep with Livia insistently voicing her displeasure with the world.

She was probably going to have trouble sleeping no matter what. There was the fire, and there was Dane. The two were not related, but Dane had made no secret of the fact that he wanted her farm, and the thought of him hovering on the peripheries waiting for her to give up on her dream made her edgy. Why was he interested in Littlegate Farm? There were lots of other small farms in the Larkspur Valley.

Should she call Derek and tell him to call off his brother? She'd rather have a root canal.

Kat stepped out onto the porch, running her hands over her upper arms. Livia was not giving in to exhaustion, and after a particularly gusty cry, Kat found herself heading down the walk toward the trailer as if guided by autopilot. Troy needed a break.

Her steps slowed as she approached the trailer. *Should* she offer to help? Another loud wail helped her decide. Yes. Otherwise no one was getting any sleep.

The windows of the little trailer were open, so instead of knocking on the door, Kat simply called Troy's name.

"Is there anything I can do?" she asked without waiting for an answer.

The trailer creaked with movement, then the door opened, and a frazzled cowboy stepped out with a red-faced quiet-for-the-moment baby in his arms.

"Are we keeping you awake?" The polite note in his voice was impressive given the circumstances. Livia let out a wail. He didn't even seem to notice.

"No. I'm just wondering if I can help. I mean, you put out a fire for me."

One that I could have put out myself...

Troy met her gaze and then nodded. He gently handed over the baby, and Kat gathered the now-silent child against her. The little girl was warm, but not fever warm, and her face was damp even though she appeared to have run out of tears.

"I don't know what the deal is," Troy said. "I've searched every baby site on the planet, and it could be a lot of things. Teething. Colic. Gas. I don't know." He pushed his hand through his hair, which was already standing on end.

"Has she done this before?"

"Never for this long."

Kat started rocking the child against her, as she had the infant that she'd babysat for during high school. Livia took great offense. Troy gave Kat a helpless look and reached for his baby, but Kat shook her head.

"I have her. You need a break."

"A short one."

"Can I come inside?"

"Yeah. Of course." He stood back so that she could mount the single aluminum step. Once inside the trailer, which was small, small, small, she took a seat on the sofa that would have folded out into a bed if the bassinet hadn't been in the way. Troy's bedroll was stashed next to the door leading to the small bathroom, and she wondered if he was sleeping on the floor of the mini kitchen or moving the bassinet out of the way in order to fold out the bed.

Kat lifted the baby higher in her arms and rocked her, murmuring soothing sounds that Livia ignored. Troy looked on with a weary expression on his handsome face.

"If you have a minute, maybe I could wash my dishes."

"Go ahead," she said, patting the baby's back. "Do dishes, take a walk. Whatever you need to do."

Troy did dishes. Livia quieted for a few minutes and then started again, only not so insistently. Kat continued to soothe her and then pulled her phone out of her pocket. "I'm calling my mom."

"It's late."

"Mom paints until eleven or twelve. It's her creative time."

Troy nodded, and Kat hit her mom's name in the contact list. Emily answered on the first ring.

"Taking a break or facing a challenge?" Kat asked. Her mom never answered this fast while she had a brush in her hand.

"My commissioned bulldog looks like Winston Churchill."

"There is a resemblance," Kat said.

"There hasn't been another fire?" Her mom's way of asking for reassurance that all was well.

"No fire. I need some baby advice."

"Okay," her mother said slowly.

"Do you know anything about inconsolable crying?"

"Teething, colic, gas. Does she have a fever?"

"I don't think so, but we'll check."

We.

"I'd guess either her gums or her belly hurts. You can't do much for the belly, but try ice chips or a frozen washcloth for the gums. It might help. You can also put her carrier on the washer when it's in a spin cycle. That worked with James, or take a long drive, which worked with the rest of you."

"Ask at what point I go to the emergency room?" Troy asked.

Emily must've heard him, "When he feels like he needs to. Tell him to follow his gut, but to try the ice chips and the drive first."

"Thanks, Mom."

"Let me know what happens."

"I will." Kat ended the call and dropped her phone on the sofa next to her. "Try ice chips in a cloth before heading to the emergency room."

"I don't have ice."

"I do." Kat eased her way to her feet and gently passed the baby to her father. "Be back in a minute."

Troy patted Livia's back as he gave Kat a tired look. "Thank you."

Kat wanted to tell him that this was what people did—they helped one another—but after a couple hours of dealing with a crying infant, she was pretty certain Troy didn't need a pep talk. Instead of imparting semi-hypocritical wisdom about accepting help when needed, she said, "Hang in there. I'll be right back."

KAT RETURNED A few minutes later with a plastic zipper bag of ice and a white washcloth. After wrapping a smallish cube in the cloth and handing it to Troy, she managed to push the bag into the ridiculously tiny freezer compartment.

"I don't know what happened to the ice

trays that used to be here, but this works," Kat said. "You can get ice from me anytime."

Livia stopped crying when Troy rubbed the cold damp cloth over her gums, and her eyes went wide, like she was considering the interesting feeling. A second later, her little hands came up to grab the cloth as she sucked on it.

"So far, so good," Troy said a split second before Livia pushed the cloth away and turned her head. He coaxed her into allowing him to run the ice over her gums again.

"I think I feel the tooth," he said.

"Hopefully, it'll break through soon and give her some relief."

"Amen to that. I guess I'll buy one of those teething things that you freeze tomorrow," he said.

"I'd buy two. One for immediate use, one for the freezer."

"Good plan."

A brief silence fell, then Kat asked, "Does she crawl?"

Troy smiled a little as Livia made slurpy

noises on the cloth. "She pushes up onto her hands and knees and rocks."

"So she's not permanently attached to your chest?"

He laughed, feeling better now that Livia wasn't as distraught. She was still thinking about crying, but in a more half-hearted way. If ice made this much of a difference, he wouldn't have to go to the emergency room.

"It probably looks that way, but she gets lots of floor time." He pointed to a folded blanket next to the bassinet with a small basket of colorful toys sitting on top of it. "She gives those rings a workout. Particularly the purple one."

Kat smiled a little and got to her feet. A shaft of disappointment shot through Troy at the thought of being alone again, but instead of saying goodbye and good luck, Kat held out her hands. "Let me take her for a while more."

Troy almost protested. Almost said he was good and that he didn't need any more help, but the words didn't come. And he didn't bother wondering why.

"Thanks." He handed his daughter over to Kat. Livia gave a small warning whimper and then set about sucking the cold cloth again. Troy, who suddenly had nothing to do, sat down and watched as Kat crooned to Livia and walked the short distance to the bathroom door and back to the bassinet, her lips curved into a gentle smile as she studied the baby's face. And when Livia pushed the cloth away and debated about crying, Kat cajoled her out of it. Part of it was the ice, part was that Livia was probably so exhausted that she didn't have the energy to really cut loose again.

Kat continued to walk the baby and Troy closed his eyes for the briefest of moments, comforted by Kat's steady footfalls and soft murmurs. Why had he felt that moment of disappointment when he'd thought she was leaving?

Because an adult needs company.

He'd had lots of that working for Grace and Herm. He'd had his own place, but they'd helped with Livia and had him over frequently. He'd given no thought to facing isolation after they sold their business and retired.

It wasn't like he was facing a unique situation. Lots of single parents dealt with similar challenges. He just needed to get his equilibrium.

Kat's footsteps continued in an even cadence as she paced and murmured, paced and murmured. Troy told himself to open his eyes, because he needed to take Livia off her hands. Relieve her of duty so that she could go back to her house and do whatever it was she did in the evenings.

Yes. He needed to do that.

Soon.

KAT HAD TWO sleeping Mackays on her hands. Troy had started softly snoring not long after she'd taken the baby from him and he'd settled on the sofa. Livia had proven more challenging. Finally, after a good twenty minutes of walking, Livia's little body had gone slack, and Kat was able to ease the wet washcloth out of her hand.

She set the cloth on the counter, ever so

gently eased the baby off her shoulder and slowly laid her on her back in the bassinet. Livia stirred, but her little eyes stayed shut, as did her father's. Excellent.

She studied the baby's angelic face, wondering how something so cute could make so much noise, then she turned and crept toward the door, wondering if she could operate the creaky handle without waking father or daughter.

"Hey." The low-spoken word rolled over her as she reached the door.

Kat turned to find Troy regarding her from the sofa. She smiled and paused with her hand on the creaky handle.

"Thanks."

There was a note of gratitude in his voice but also something that made it more difficult to open the door and leave.

"Anytime. And I mean that."

He nodded, but she knew that he wouldn't voluntarily call on her unless things got rough. Really rough.

She hesitated, escape no longer a priority. "Ask for help when you need it."

He gave a small shrug in reply. "I guess I have a thing about owing people."

"Why's that?" She was curious whether his motivations were similar to her own. She didn't want to be manipulated and controlled. Did he fear the same thing?

Livia stirred before Troy could answer, and Kat and Troy went comically still until the baby let out a sigh and settled again. Troy eased himself off the sofa and edged past the bassinet. Kat opened the door, and he followed her into the unseasonably warm evening.

Once outside, they walked a few feet away from the trailer to where they could speak in more normal voices, and by that time, she realized that asking personal questions might not be her best move—even if she was curious about this gorgeous man. "Forget I asked. It's none of my business."

"It's okay." Troy ran a hand over the back of his neck and then dropped it again. "It's not that I don't want help."

"Then what?" The questions that she didn't mean to ask just kept coming.

One corner of his mouth tightened as he

met her gaze. "The more I can handle on my own, the less dependent I'll be on something that might disappear tomorrow."

"Troy Mackay against the world," Kat said softly.

"You make it sound like I'm tilting at windmills." He shifted his weight, put a hand on one hip as he glanced past Kat. "Okay. Here's the thing. I need help."

Her eyebrows went up. "What kind of help?"

"A lady called me about a shoeing job, but I don't want to book anyone without having childcare in place." She gave him a curious look, and he said, "Having Livia on the job didn't work out well. One of my clients had to push her in a stroller today so that I could work."

"Which one?"

"Walt—"

"Walt Stenson? You had cranky Walt pushing a stroller?"

"Yeah. I'd kind of like to not do that again."

A slow smile spread across her face. "Are you asking me to babysit?"

"Not if it interferes with your work, but…yes. I am asking."

Frankly, she was honored, because obviously, Troy didn't trust just anyone with his baby. She was also in her comfort zone. Helping others deal with trouble was something she'd done since she was a child, thanks to Andrew, Kent and James.

"I'm happy to babysit, Troy. When?"

"I'd like to book the job for the day after tomorrow."

"That works perfectly."

"And it doesn't squeeze you for time?"

She gave an innocent shake of her head. "I do my day job at night."

"As one does."

"As this one does. It gives me time to work on the fences in the daylight."

"I can help you with that. The fences, not the daylight."

"I'm good," she said a bit too airily.

"Are you sure?"

"Why wouldn't I be?" Now there was a faintly defensive edge to her voice.

"I thought we agreed that I would help while I was here."

"With the heavy lifting," she clarified. Because he had his own job to attend to.

"Fencing doesn't involve heavy lifting?"

"Nothing that I can't handle. I have a little less than two weeks to get things ready for my first clients. I can manage, though." She gave him a look. "You know, like I would have if Arlie hadn't cheated you."

"That wasn't the deal."

She gave him a gentle scowl. "It is the deal."

"You babysit for me, and I do nothing for you?"

Kat let out a sigh. "Yes. That's it."

"I'm helping with the fences."

Kat pushed out her chin. "We'll see."

The look he gave her was as stubborn as any that she'd ever gotten from her brothers. "Why are you so afraid of asking for help, Kat?"

She opened her mouth. Closed it again. That was not a question she cared to answer, and the irony did not escape her. Finally, she said, "When I need help, I'll ask for it."

It wasn't a total untruth. She *would* ask

in a serious situation, like in a fire. But if she handled things alone, life would be less complicated. She would be less tempted to make it more complicated. The thought of working shoulder to shoulder with Troy was enticing in a sweaty-cowboy-no-shirt kind of way, which was why she had to squelch it.

"I'll hold you to that." His mouth quirked on one side. "And in the meantime, I appreciate you babysitting." He gave her a look that made her midsection do a tiny freefall. "And that, Kat Farley, is how one accepts help, even when they don't want to."

CHAPTER EIGHT

DEW ON THE thick grass dampened Kat's shoes and jeans as she pushed open the pasture gate and walked back to her idling truck. The sun was up, but just barely, and the breeze carried the scent of evergreens and blooming clover. Kat inhaled, loving the beauty, the serenity of her new home. Littlegate Farm. Home. It was a good feeling.

The meadow grass was tall and ripe, perfect for grazing, and she drove along the periphery of the fence she'd be working on, so as to crush as little as possible. If she got the boarding contract for the Tennessee walkers, she'd have to procure hay to feed in addition to the grass pasture, and the feeders needed a good scrub with the pressure washer, more for appearances than anything else.

She would have liked to have had time

to paint the barn and start the many improvements she had in mind, but she didn't. Littlegate Farm was showing its age, but with secure fences, a sturdy horse barn that would be painted in the not-so-distant future, small pole corrals, clean feeders and new water tanks, Kat believed she had a facility that would pass muster—unless the Tennessee walker people were persnickety. That said, when she'd spoken with Ada at OPM, it sounded as if the people were easy to work with.

One could hope, but if she didn't have sturdy, horse-friendly fences, she was not going to be able to take on boarders, thus the early morning start. She figured that by putting in a few hours every morning before the heat set in, she'd get the job done without help from her tenant, who'd politely and ironically demonstrated how to accept help even when it went against the grain.

Well, he had a baby to think of. She had herself. She was in a less tenuous position than he was, and she didn't need to ask—

What the—?

Kat abruptly stopped the truck on top of the gently rolling hill that hid the back pasture fence from the rest of the farm. All the work she'd done the previous day had been destroyed. The wire that had been stretched tautly between wooden posts was now detached and lying in lazy coils that extended into the pasture.

It looked like something had hit the fence from the outside and stretched the wire inward until it came loose from the posts and broke.

Kat eased the truck forward, following her tracks from the previous day. As she got closer to the fence, she could clearly see indications that someone had driven a vehicle through the fence that bordered the rear of Littlegate Farm directly into her pasture. There was no way anyone driving that road would be going fast enough to lose control and drive through a fence. Was there?

All indicators pointed to yes, because the evidence was before her. At least the posts were still standing, but it was going to be a job replacing and reattaching the smooth wire.

"Argh." Kat smacked the steering wheel. If she didn't get mad, she was probably going to get sick, because her stomach was turning itself inside out.

This was crazy. The outhouse fire, which looked accidental, and now this...accident. Coincidence?

It had to be, but what if it wasn't? Would Dane be gutsy enough to do something like this and risk his good name if he were caught? Kat didn't see that happening, which caused a frisson of relief to go through her. A couple of random smacks from the universe she could deal with. Being targeted... That was a different matter.

She got out of the truck and started walking the fence line. The soft morning breeze caressed her face and lifted her hair. A perfect morning to work, only she hadn't counted on this much of it.

Kat picked up a detached strand of wire, lifting it to see how badly it had tangled back on itself. She dropped it with a sinking feeling. Yesterday's long day had been for nothing, with the exception of the two rotting fence posts she'd replaced. Kat put a hand on the nearest post and shook it. It was reasonably tight. The weather would tamp the earth around it, but the wire…

She turned and went back to her truck with a purposeful stride. She needed to get another roll of wire and the big stretcher and tackle this mess. She was a Farley. They bounced back.

They also had to buy wire. When Kat returned to the ranch and went to the area behind the machine shed where the posts and wire were stored, she found drag marks instead of what was supposed to be there.

Heart beating faster, Kat pushed her hair back from her forehead as she studied the few bent recycled T-posts that remained. Okay…this was harder to mark as an accident. In fact, it seemed pretty darned deliberate.

LIVIA WOKE UP HAPPY, cooing and smiling her wide baby smile as she sat up in the portable crib, alternately waving her arms and putting toys in her mouth. Troy lifted her from the crib and lightly ran the tip of his finger over her bottom gum where he felt two teeth breaking through. Maybe the worst was over. For now. Soon another tooth would start working its way to the surface, and he'd have another parenting adventure. Thanks to Kat and her mom, he hadn't headed to the ER for a toothache.

He'd heard Kat drive her truck into the pasture early that morning while he'd been reading his phone and waiting for his exhausted baby to stir. She'd come back not long after, and when he glanced out the trailer window when Livia made her first morning coo, he saw the truck parked in its usual spot. So much for his theory that she was going to work on the fences early so that she could do it without him offering to help.

Fat chance. If she was going to babysit for him, he was helping her. Quid pro quo and all that.

He knew why he had issues with dependency, but what had happened with Kat? He doubted that she could trace things to her family situation as he could to his. Her family might be a touch wild, or so he'd heard, but they were obviously supportive. So…nature rather than nurture? And why was he so curious?

He wasn't going to lie to himself. He was attracted to Kat, which was something he was going to have to work around. She'd made it very clear after they'd kissed that she had regrets, and the last thing he was going to do was give her more regrets while simultaneously complicating his own life.

Troy fed his baby, changed her diaper and dressed her in a long-sleeved giraffe Onesie with matching pants. After that, he headed across the driveway to Kat's house to firm up the babysitting plan. Livia babbled and tugged at the brim of his ball cap as they walked across the driveway, making him smile when the cap dipped over his eye and almost came off. He caught it and popped it onto her head only to have her pull it off again and hold it in both hands.

The front door of Kat's house was open, and after he knocked on edge of the old-fashioned wooden screen door, she called for him to come in.

"In the kitchen," she added unnecessarily, since he could see her sitting at the table with her laptop pushed to one side and a yellow legal pad in front of her. She looked up as he entered the room and tried to smile, but the uptilt of his lips barely qualified.

"What's wrong?" he asked.

"Just pricing fencing."

There was a dark edge to her voice that he didn't understand. He took a seat, holding Livia on his lap. She squirmed to get off, so he set her on her stomach on the floor. She pushed up to her hands and knees and rocked.

The three of them sat in silence in the small kitchen, Livia staring up at Troy with her drooly grin and Kat's gaze focusing on the legal pad.

"Kat…maybe it's time to tell me what's going on."

She gave him a grim look and stood up. "Do you and Livia want to walk with me?"

"Sure."

He scooped up his baby, mystified as to where they were going. A few minutes later, they passed the charred remains of the outhouse and continued on to a long low shed that housed the tractors. Kat walked around the shed, stopped, and pointed at three bent T-posts.

"This is what is left of my fencing supplies."

"Okay…" He had no idea where this was going.

"Yesterday, I had at least ten wooden posts, two bundles of new T-posts and at least three big rolls of wire."

Troy lifted Livia higher in his arms as he studied the drag marks where someone had obviously made off with Kat's fencing supplies.

"Random theft?" He hated the idea of thieves in the area. Littlegate Farm was isolated, one of two properties on a lonely road, and the other property was currently vacant, according to Walt.

"I truly doubt it." She pushed back her hair as she turned to him. "The fence that I fixed yesterday was ripped out. It could've been an accident. It's close to a maintenance road, and someone could have lost control of their vehicle and then simply driven away."

"And the fire is supposed to have been an accident." He poked the bent T-post with the toe of his boot. "The missing materials—not an accident."

"My ex's brother wants Littlegate Farm."

Troy's head came up at the stark announcement. "That's the guy in the Land Rover? The one with the offer that would benefit you both?"

"The same."

"I knew I didn't like the guy."

Kat merely nodded as she studied the drag marks. Troy shifted his weight. Waited. Kat obviously hadn't had a lot of practice spilling her guts, and since he was the same way, he felt her pain as she worked through the process. Finally, she raised her gaze.

"The farm is the reason I broke up with Derek—the brother of the guy who wants my farm."

"Is this Derek guy a local?"

"He still lives in Washington. We graduated high school together but didn't start dating until college. After that, we both took jobs in Spokane." She frowned as if remembering something. "I wanted to go to work in Missoula, but he talked me into Spokane." She gave her head a rueful shake. "He talked me into or out of a lot of things. And I let him."

"What kind of things?"

"The farm for one. Well, almost. After my aunt offered it to me, he made excellent points as to why it was a white elephant and how I would better off if I let it go. I was this close—" she held up her thumb and forefinger with a tiny space between them "—to doing just that when I overheard him on the phone talking to Dane. He told his brother that he'd just about convinced me to give up the place." She gave him a look. "He said that I always came around to his way of thinking. That I was compliant."

"You?"

"Yes." The word came out grimly.

"That seems...out of character."

"Thank you for that." Kat gave a little snort. "But he was right. I had this idea in my head of what a grown-up normal life was like." She managed a wry smile that faded a split second later. "It was pretty much the opposite of my family life. I wanted predictability and stability, and I assumed that meant compromise. So when Derek and I disagreed, I usually gave in. I never realized how often...or how good he was at manipulating me." Another rueful shake of her head. "After growing up with my brothers, I thought I was too smart to be manipulated or fooled. You can't believe how many times I had to sniff out a plot to save one of them from themselves..." She pulled in a breath. "I digress."

"Do you think this Dane guy could be behind the fencing theft?" Because if there was someone creeping around the place while his daughter was in residence, he was going to have to do something about it.

"It's the only thing that makes sense. He made a veiled threat about things happening when I last spoke to him. I thought it was masculine pride talking." She made a face. "The Cashman brothers have a lot of masculine pride."

"What's his game? Does he think that

stealing a few fence posts is going to put you out of business?"

"I think he thinks that he can make things difficult for me. And if they get too difficult—or creepy—that I'll cut and run, and he can snap up the place."

"Could that happen?"

"I have no more cows to sell, my parents aren't in a position to float a private loan, and after purchasing the farm, my credit is stretched to the max—"

"That's a yes."

She nodded. "Total yes. The thing I can't figure is how he did it when between the two of us, someone was home for most of the day yesterday."

"A utility truck came by yesterday when Livia and I were heading out."

"What kind of utility?"

"Electric. Maybe plumbing. I thought it was your friend Sparky—"

"Squeak."

"Right. Checking on some electrical thing."

"Did you see the driver? Was it a woman?"

"The truck shot past me in a big cloud of dust."

"Interesting." Kat shot him a sidelong look. "If someone drove a utility truck onto the property, and one of us was home, it'd be easy to ask for directions, wouldn't it? Happens all the time in a rural area."

"And if we weren't at home, that would give them an opportunity to steal fencing supplies."

"Crazy theory," Kat said. But it was obvious that she was a believer.

"And creepy, like you said." He hoisted Livia higher in his arms.

Kat must have noted the unconsciously protective move, because she said, "Dane might want my property, but I don't believe he'd go so far as to hurt anyone. Not physically," she added. "It would ruin me emotionally to lose my farm."

"What about the fire?"

"I don't know," she admitted. "You saw the wiring. That could have been an actual accident."

"Maybe so, but I don't want to take a chance. Not with Livia here." *And not with you.* "Even if the fire was a fluke, this other stuff was not." He met her gaze. "Should we confront this guy?"

Kat started to give him a *This is not your problem* look and then seemed to think better of it. "He's litigious. All I need is for him to come up with a reason to sue me."

"Which he may yet do."

"If I give cause, which I will be very careful not to do." She pulled in a deep breath. "We have no proof of anything except for a theft of post and wire."

"Are you going to contact law enforcement?"

She made an incredulous face. "Not for a piddling wire-and-post theft. My brothers will get wind of it, and I'll have one camped here to protect me."

"That may not be a bad thing."

"I have you," she said simply. "I don't need an extra guard. Not that you're a guard. Or that I need you." She pulled in a frustrated breath. "How about I just shut up now?"

"Let's talk about fences. When do you take the Tennessee walker people through the facility?"

"Late next week." She cleared her throat. "Troy… I appreciate the help, but—"

"You're afraid I'm going to try to take over or something?"

"I've been burned before."

Her lips parted slightly as their gazes locked, and he suspected that the real issue was that she was as drawn to him as he was to her…and that after her last experience, she wasn't about to take a chance on him or any other man.

He understood better than she knew.

"I'm going to ask you to let me help you get your place ready for those horses. In return, I'm also going to ask you to lend a hand with Livia when it doesn't get in the way of your other work."

"So kind of a trade-off deal." She could live with that.

"A limited partnership."

He touched her cheek with the back of his hand, and Livia reached for her hair, but he managed to keep her from grabbing.

"I'm a solo act, Kat, as are you."

"I need to be on my own," she agreed. "At least until I trust my judgment again."

She grimaced. "I was almost a Stepford wife."

He touched her cheek again, this time with his palm, slid a hand around the back of her neck and leaned in to kiss her as he balanced Livia against his shoulder. Kat met his lips with a kiss that was both quick and sweet. The sealing of a deal.

"Is that an acknowledgment of our limited partnership?"

"Beats a handshake," he said easily.

"You make a good point." She eased back half a step, and he was glad to see her lips form a wry smile. Kat might feel drawn to him, as he was to her, but she wasn't going to let her guard down. Not even when a spark or two flew between them.

"As soon as Littlegate Farm is ready for horses and I start my new job and find another place to live, we'll be people who bump into each other at the grocery store."

That felt like a lie, but it was what gun-shy Kat needed to hear. And honestly, it was the scenario that would be best for them both.

"I can live with that," she said.

So could he…even though hearing the words spoken aloud made his heart sink.

Tough.

Sometimes the heart had to change its mind about what it wanted.

TROY HAD BEEN justifiably nervous about leaving Livia alone with Kat on the farm after the string of odd incidents, so Kat had arranged a girls' day in the park with Maddie.

"I can't believe I'm able to get away from the shop in June," her friend said as she flopped down on the striped picnic blanket Kat had spread out under an ancient elm tree.

"I was going to ask how you managed," Kat said. "Then decided that I didn't want to know." There'd been times where Maddie had been stretched to the limit and had threatened to hang a "Gone Fishing" sign on the boutique window, lock the door and disappear.

Maddie shifted her yellow chiffon skirt to cover her knees as she sat cross-legged.

"Kayla's niece, Elsa, is putting in a few hours now that she's on break from school."

"That has to help."

"So much." Maddie leaned close to Livia, who instantly started sticking out her bottom lip.

"Oh," Maddie said, easing back. "Stranger danger?"

Kat nodded as the little girl snuggled against her, giving Maddie a suspicious eye. But the boo-boo lip had disappeared, so yay for that.

"Aren't you the honored one?"

"I am." Kat bent her head to breath in the sweet smell of baby and feel the soft tickle of downy hair against her cheek."

"I'm envious."

"This was slow to happen, but…"

"The babysitting or the baby not being afraid of you?"

"Both, to be honest." Kat rocked the little girl against her as Maddie opened the small cooler of sandwiches she'd brought along. "Daisy Lane has limited openings. I think Troy prefers to use the daycare center, but he's been getting a lot of calls for jobs and doesn't want to turn them down."

"So he needs you."

"Yes." Kat took a sandwich and maneuvered the wrapper off with one hand. "And it looks like I need him for a while, too."

"How so?"

Kat took a bite, and after swallowing, she filled her friend in on the fire, the fence and the theft.

"Holy…" Maddie's eyes were round by the time Kat had finished. "Do you think you're in danger?"

"The fire is concerning, but it's the only one of the three that could be a legitimate accident. You should have seen those wires."

"The other things sound like the penny-ante stuff that Dane would pull. But it's still nothing to ignore." Maddie slowly chewed her sandwich and then took a drink of water. "Why is he so gung ho to get the place? Commission?"

"I think he might have had a buyer waiting in the wings, and I messed up the deal. But it isn't like I have the only small farm in the area. I looked online this morning, and there are several that are in better shape than Littlegate Farm, and the prices aren't that bad." Although everything had gone up over the past several years.

"Maybe he's just ticked that you didn't fall into line as expected and is teaching you a lesson. Making a point, so to speak."

"Well, I doubt that he was driving the utility truck. He wouldn't risk that."

"But he might know someone who would. Too bad Troy didn't get the name off the side."

"I know. I've asked James if he knows anyone who works for a company that would have a truck and might be open to some nefarious work."

"How did that go?" Maddie asked with genuine interest.

"It was a difficult conversation. On the one hand, if anyone would have that information, it would be James. People talk to him. On the other, I had to have a legitimate reason for asking that didn't put him in protective-brother mode."

"How'd you do it?"

Kat laughed. "I pretended I wanted to hire a guy to jury-rig a satellite TV dish."

Maddie grinned appreciatively.

"The kicker is that he talked me out of it. Told me it isn't worth the risk."

"What are the risks?"

"I don't know. The thing is, James doesn't know of anyone like that, plumbers or electricians."

"And he was focused on keeping his little sister out of trouble," Maddie said wryly.

"Right." Kat glanced down to see that Livia's eyes had drifted shut. She held the baby a little closer and continued to gently rock.

Maddie's gaze followed the movement. "She's sweet."

"And her dad is hot." Kat figured that part was coming up next. "We have decided to form a partnership. The platonic kind. I'll babysit when the daycare is unavailable, and he'll help me fix the fences. I don't have a lot of time before the Tennessee walker people stop by, and I want to put up some advertising. The quicker I get the place in shape, the sooner I'll get some relief on the mortgage."

"Cutting things close?"

"They're manageable now, but if my fences keep getting destroyed, then yes, I'll be cutting things very close."

"I'm glad he's there," Maddie said, leaning back on her elbows and stretching her legs in front of her. "Your cowboy."

So was Kat, but she was leery of becoming dependent on the man. She didn't really know him…even though it felt as if she did. Why was that?

It was a question she'd mulled over more than once. Every time she let it go, it cropped up again after a Troy encounter.

"You should meet him."

"Why?"

"I need a read," Kat said honestly. "After Derek, I'll be asking for second opinions for a while."

"Are you…interested?"

Kat's gaze flashed up. "No." The word came out too quickly. Maddie's eyebrows rose, and Kat launched into damage control. "What I mean is that yes, he's super attractive. And as I'm sure Whit has told you, I kissed him. But neither of us are interested in…." She made a gesture.

"Anything?" Maddie finished for her.

"Exactly." She stroked the now sleeping baby's back. "We discussed things, and we agreed that we'll have a cooperative arrangement while Troy is on the ranch, and when he goes, then that's that."

"A cooperative arrangement," Maddie said in a mildly skeptical tone.

"Fencing and babysitting. Farm repairs and…babysitting." Kat cleared her throat. Why did it sound like she was trying to convince herself?

She shifted the baby so that her arm didn't go to sleep.

"I know how easily this could get out of hand," she confessed. "But frankly, I need him, and he needs me. As long as we're honest and keep communicating… I think we'll be okay. And maybe by the time Troy moves on, Dane will have gotten over his snit."

"That's what you think it is?"

"I have to hope it is."

"If it's not?"

Kat once again inhaled the sweet scent of baby and then shook her head. "I don't know, Maddie. I guess I have to take it one day at a time."

Just as she was going to take working with Troy one day at a time. He was attractive but not irresistible—right?

Unfortunately, her small voice refused to reply.

"Is everything okay?"

"Yeah," Troy said, glancing up at the owner of the Morgan mare he was fitting shoes to.

"You look so serious. I thought there might be a problem with the hoof."

"Nope. Her feet look good." He set the mare's hoof on the ground and ran a hand down her shoulder before walking to his truck and pulling out a double-aught shoe to try on for size.

The truth was that he was concerned, but it had nothing to do with the horse. Kat said she had babysitting experience, but he wasn't used to spending time away from his daughter, so of course he was on edge. That said, he trusted that if there were any issues, Kat would text him. So far, his phone had remained blessedly silent.

The mare was easy, just as the woman had promised over the phone, and while he shod the horse, the lady—Judy, if he remembered right—regaled him with a bit of light gossip and asked his opinion about various shoeing techniques—hot forge, cold, glue-on. He maintained his end of the conversation, finished the mare in record time and then thanked her for her business.

"I'll be recommending you to my friends," she said. "Thanks for working me in."

"Not a problem." He started putting away his gear.

"Have you thought of advertising on social media?"

He hadn't, but it was a decent idea.

"I only say that because I saw your ad on the bulletin board at the feedstore, but when I went back the next day to get your number, it was gone. I tried the grocery store and the community bulletin board and couldn't find anything. The only reason I was able to find you was because I knew you'd done Patricia's horses."

"Huh." Because he'd definitely left ads in all those places. "Guess you're right. I should put something online." He put the last of the tools away and closed the tailgate. "This will eventually be a side gig. I start driving for L&S in the fall."

"Will you keep me on your client list?"

"You bet."

On the way back to the farm, Troy swung by the feedstore. Sure enough, his ad was missing. He checked for other farrier ads, thinking that a jealous local might not have wanted him cutting in on his business, but there were none. Maybe someone had wanted his services all to themselves.

Unlikely.

There was nothing he could do except to bring new ads to town when he came back and to put something up on social media.

Word of mouth was often enough in the farrier world, especially if a guy demonstrated that he could handle the rougher equine customers. Soon he'd be driving and not dependent solely on farrier work. He'd do all right. It was Kat he was worried about.

He would be leaving Littlegate Farm in the near future...but not while odd things were happening there. Kat could use assistance, and after all she'd done to help him, he couldn't have not offered to partner with her. While he was on Littlegate Farm, they would be a team. If this Cashman guy was working against Kat, he'd also have to contend with Troy.

"WE DID GREAT." Kat smiled as Livia reached for her daddy, who took her and nuzzled her cheek.

"Did you have a good day?" he asked the baby. Livia gave a happy squeal. Troy shifted her in his arms and turned toward Kat. "All went well?"

"For us."

"Meaning?"

"Were *you* a wreck being away from your little girl?"

"A little bit." And he refused to feel bad about it. "First time separated in a long time, but I know it's good for her to experience new things."

"How did you manage to drive trucks when she was a newborn?"

"Grace, the owner, watched Livia for me. She was very grandmotherly."

"What a sweet deal."

"You have no idea. I knew nothing about babies. I mean, I'd read books and articles, but the reality… Let's just say that I was fortunate to be mentored by someone who's been through it." He lifted Livia in the air and blew a raspberry on her tummy. She laughed, and he set her back against his shoulder.

"I brought the beer." He nodded at the bag he'd set on the table.

"Then I guess I'll do my part and make the hot dogs." She grinned at him over her shoulder. "In case you're wondering, I have more than hot dogs in my repertoire. Once I get my kitchen all the way unpacked, I can make hamburgers and spaghetti, too."

"I can grill a steak and cook a burger, but I generally eat a lot of frozen and microwave stuff."

"Bachelor life?"

"And rodeo life. But once Button is on solid food, I'll have to start looking at healthier options."

Kat met Troy's gaze and smiled. She headed for the kitchen, and he touched her arm, stopping her as she passed.

"You doing okay?" he asked, because something seemed just a little off.

"Fine." He held her gaze until she said in an overly offhand way, "I might have dropped by Dane's office again on my way to buy fencing supplies."

"With Livia?" Because if so…

"Maddie sat in the truck with her when I went in. Livia likes Maddie, and you know that I would never put your daughter in a situation like that." She sounded a touch insulted.

"I don't like *you* confronting him, either."

Stating the first thought that struck him after finding out that Livia had been well cared for had been an error. Kat's eyebrows almost touched her hairline.

"I can't help but feel protective," he added.

"My brothers are protective. It's smothering. I thought Derek was protective, but it was a way to control me." She pointed a finger at his chest. "I don't need protecting."

"All right, then maybe *you* can protect *me* while I'm on the property."

For a moment, she simply stared at him, then she rolled her eyes and turned away, but not before he caught the smile.

"How did the showdown go?"

"No showdown." Her voice was now close to normal, the nerve he'd touched assuaged. "He was out. But I left a message that I don't think he can use as the basis for a lawsuit."

"Which was…?"

"I said I thought he might be interested in my property improvements, that I've installed cameras."

Troy gave an impressed laugh. "Nice. Then what?"

"I followed through. Ate a big hole in my budget, but I thought it was worth it. I could only afford two. Squeak is going to help me set them up."

"It's ridiculous that you had to do that."

"You need to understand something about the Cashman family. They make the rules." She lifted her eyebrows in a significant expression. "I'm breaking them."

He touched her again, and she looked up, only this time, he allowed his fingers to linger on her shoulder.

"And that's why I can't help but feel protective."

He let his hand drop as Kat moved away. She pulled a pan out of the dishrack, filled it with water to boil hotdogs, put it on a flame, then started opening a can of baked beans.

"Do your best to rein it in, okay?" She spoke mildly, and it was the mildness that convinced him of how serious she was.

"Why does he want your place?"

"I don't know," Kat said as she cut open the pack of hotdogs. "I've asked him, but I got no answer to speak of. Surprise, surprise." She shot him a look over her shoulder. "Short of buried treasure, I can't come up with a reason he specifically wants it."

"Nothing new going on anywhere? Highway going through or something?"

She grinned. "Oh, yeah. A major highway right past my place to dead-end on the mountain behind the Bealmans."

"No gold prospects, no potential for... anything?"

"Nothing."

Troy came to join her at the counter, using his free hand to dump the open can of beans into the pan she'd set beside it. He tossed the baked bean can into the trash, set a squirming Livia on the floor and handed her the set of measuring spoons Kat had left out. Livia's mouth made an O as she reached for the spoons, and once they were in her chubby fist, she started shaking them.

"When do the cameras go in?" he asked as Kat put the pan of beans on a rear burner.

"Squeak said she'd have time tomorrow."

"Good. I just hope the message gets through to Mr. Cashman."

"Me too."

Livia let out a happy squeal and threw the spoons in the air. Kat smiled and turned back to the stove, but Troy sensed she still had something on her mind. A moment later, she broke the silence.

"I appreciate having you here, Troy. I truly do. But don't feel like you have to stay if something else comes along."

Troy went still. "What are you saying, Kat?"

She met his gaze. "I'm saying that I like having you here. I don't *need* to have you here."

He begged to differ.

Until he was certain that Cashman had backed off, he did need to be here. But there was no way that he was going to ruin the moment and alienate Kat by saying those words aloud.

So instead he bent down to pick up his daughter from the floor, wrinkling his nose as she grabbed at it, then turning her in his arms so that they both faced Kat.

"You know what?" he asked softly.

She shook her head. "I don't."

"Protective issues aside, I want to be here.

It works." And because she still wore a faint frown, he added, "For now."

Kat's brow cleared, and his heart sank a little, even though it had no business doing that. They were in a temporary business-like relationship for all the right reasons. He needed to accept that…but he couldn't help thinking that it would be easier to do that if he didn't feel such a deep longing for the woman.

"I was just making sure…" Kat gestured, and then her tone shifted as she said, "Last time I make that point. Promise."

"Right," he said with a gentle smirk.

The word had the effect he'd hoped for, and Kat made a face before giving his arm a light punch.

"We're good?" he asked.

She gave a nod. "We're good."

For now.

CHAPTER NINE

"I WISH I had time to help you with the fences," Maddie said over speaker phone while Kat gathered her gloves, bandana and hat. "And since I can't, I'm glad you have Troy there."

"I think you have enough on your plate without adding fencing to the mix," Kat said.

"Planning a wedding *is* ridiculously time consuming, even knowing the ropes and having Kayla's niece spell me at the store."

"Cody is lending a hand, right?"

"He's been slammed at work, but he helps when he can. Changing the subject—" Maddie put a smile in her voice "—I was hoping to book your farrier."

"Troy?"

"Do you have another farrier on the premises?"

"It was the 'your' part that I was wondering about." Or maybe she was touchy about words that seemed to link them in anything except the most casual sense, and she shouldn't be. She was in control. Not Derek. Not Troy. She had a handle on her life, and she wasn't sharing—not the control part anyway. She didn't mind company, as long as they observed her boundaries, and last night she'd reiterated her boundary and Troy hadn't argued with her. She liked having him there, but she didn't need him there.

"Well…"

Kat could totally picture Maddie's characteristic nose wrinkle as her friend spoke.

"He's kind of yours."

"I'd say he's his own man." He might be all about protecting her, but ironically, he wasn't going to give anyone a foothold in his life. It was that realization that had finally allowed Kat to relax a little.

They both had boundaries to be observed. With Troy, she'd found someone whose needs meshed surprisingly well with her own, and when the time came, they would go their separate ways. No harm. No foul. Maybe some nice memories. Maybe they could even have a goodbye date night to celebrate the end of their partnership. That would be very civilized. Kat bit her lip at the thought and turned her attention back to the phone.

"I'll talk to Troy and get back to you. You'll need him to come on a Sunday, right?" Maddie worked six days a week in the boutique. She was supposed to take a day off midweek and leave the store in the hands of her partner, but as near as Kat could tell, that rarely happened.

"Yes, on a Sunday."

"I'll get back to you."

"Great. Thank you."

Troy was waiting by the pickup when Kat came out of the house, and she had to admit that seeing him standing there waiting for her made her heart beat a little fast. But just a little. He was her temporary helpmate, and the fact that he was easy on the eyes was both a blessing and a distraction. She liked to tell herself that she was impervious to his charms, but that was, of course, a lie. He was a great kisser, and being close to him made her feel just that much more alive.

And that's exactly how you got into trouble with Derek. You liked that feeling a little too much.

She brushed the thought aside, because she knew the warning signs and would not succumb top such folly again. More importantly, she and Troy had an end date. He would help her and move on. She would help him until he left. She did not need to overthink things, and the realization was remarkably freeing.

"Good news?" he asked.

"For you, maybe." She tucked a thumb in her belt loop. "My friend Maddie wants to book you if you can fit her in on a Sunday."

His eyes crinkled a little at the corners, doing things to Kat that she preferred to ignore.

"I guess that depends if I have a sitter."

"You do. Speaking of which…" Kat glanced at her watch, a thick leather strap affair she wore while doing ranch work so that she could leave her phone in the truck. "We have five hours until you pick up

Livia." Troy had taken her to Daisy Lane for her first day of childcare.

Troy pulled his phone out of his pocket. "Four hours, fifty minutes."

"But who's counting?" Kat asked.

"I am." Troy smiled a little as he opened the driver's side door for her, then he walked around the truck to get into the passenger seat. "But I guess I'd better get used to it."

Truth be told, Kat missed Livia, too. She'd babysat the previous day when Troy had gotten another out-of-the-blue call, and she and Livia had engaged in some quality snuggle time, play time and a nice long cry that had ended in a nap.

Instead of trying to put the baby down without waking her or working on her computer one-handed, Kat had given in to the moment and rocked the little girl until Troy returned to the farm. She could honestly say that it was the first time in a long time that she'd been utterly locked into the moment. The future could wait, and the past didn't need to be rehashed.

It was the same sort of feeling she got

when she and Troy kissed. She knew it had an expiration date, so she wanted to enjoy it while she had it and then step away when it was done. She could trust Troy in a way that she couldn't trust Derek, but she couldn't shake the feeling that she couldn't trust herself.

She'd been wrong once, and the possibility of being wrong about someone she cared about again was unthinkable.

So she wasn't going there.

TROY'S SHOULDERS ACHED from pounding in T-posts, but he was glad to be getting back in shape. Not that he'd lost that much, but his training time had diminished after Livia's birth, and he needed to step it up again. They were also working under a deadline.

Kat had slapped up some handwritten ads and been stunned when she'd gotten immediate calls from people looking for a place to keep their horses. Two were temporary arrangements. There were people in the process of building who needed a place for their livestock until they were done. The other call had been from Patricia Knox, who was looking for a place where her Arabians wouldn't be cooped up in small pens waiting for daily exercise. She was shopping around for a larger property, and in the meanwhile, she'd decided that her babies needed room to run.

"By the way, *your* ad is still up." Troy pushed his cowboy hat back and opened the cooler to take out a bottle of water. "I checked when I drove by the feedstore on my way to Daisy Lane this morning."

"Guess yours were torn down by a jealous farrier."

"Maybe, but I don't know why. There's more than enough work to go around." The thing about farrier work was that bending over and wrestling the horse for control of its foot tended to break a body down. There were tricks to the trade, certain positions that were less harmful to the back, but it was still exhausting work, and the potential for injury was always there.

He tipped back the water for a long drink and surveyed the long stretch of fence they had yet to tackle. "When I start driving, there'll be even more work for the other farriers."

"Maybe they don't know you're going to start driving."

"I don't think there's much in this community that's unknown."

"Yeah? Then why was Dane so hot to get my place?"

He noted that she used the past tense. Almost a week had passed since Kat's fencing supplies had been stolen, and since nothing else had happened on that front, he saw that she was slowly relaxing.

But she wasn't quite there.

"That, I don't know. And so as not to tip your hand, I haven't asked."

They didn't get as far with the fencing as they'd hoped. But by the time they had to stop so that Troy could pick up Livia, they'd covered a good amount of ground.

"Any chance you could get your brothers to help tomorrow?" He had a job and hated to leave her with a deadline and no help. He also hated to leave her alone on the place, even though nothing weird had happened in several days—not since she'd told Dane Cashman about the cameras.

"Maybe," Kat said on an easy note. Too easy? As in, I'm-placating-you easy.

He narrowed his eyes as he shot her a look, but she kept her gaze front and center.

"Is there a reason you don't want to ask your brothers?"

"There's only one in the area. James. Andrew is in Wyoming, and Kent is in eastern Montana." She gave him a quick look. "James can be hard to work with."

"Why's that?"

"He knows one speed."

"Exhausting?"

"And sometimes destructive. That said, he's twenty-six this month, so maybe he's outgrown some of that. I don't think he's been to the hospital recently, so…yeah." She pursed her lips thoughtfully. "I could ask him."

"You're lucky to have a family," Troy said, glancing out the side window as they followed a faint track around the edge of the hayfield. He didn't know much about hay, but it looked ready to cut.

"Trust me. I know that." She slowed to ease through a small stream. "My brothers drove me nuts, but I can't imagine being an only child like you were."

"It's probably not bad in normal circumstances."

"What about in your circumstances?"

He thought for a moment. "Now that I'm a dad, I don't understand my parents' attitude. I would do anything for Livia."

"They didn't do…stuff…for you?"

"We didn't get a lot of one-on-one time," Troy said. "The more independent I became, the less I saw of my parents, until I rarely saw them at all." He cleared his throat. "They were…busy."

"That's awful."

"Before Livia, I might have said it didn't bother me, but—"

"It made you jump off cliffs and out of airplanes."

Definitely.

"I guess I wonder about their mindset," he said in a moment of candid confession. "I mean, how can you just ignore your kid?"

"I don't know," she replied softly. "I can

honestly say that I was never ignored. Do you have contact with your parents now?"

"Very little since I was eighteen."

"No holidays at home?"

"They were usually overseas during the big holidays. Tiff and I eloped in Vegas, so they weren't at the wedding and did not acknowledge it. When I texted them about Livia, I got a quick congrats, and that was it."

"I'm sorry you have to deal with that."

He didn't know if she was offering sympathy or simply making appropriate noises. Whichever it was, it ended the conversation until they rolled up to the parking spot beside the barn. Kat turned off the ignition but didn't move from the driver's seat.

"I didn't mean to pry."

He gave her an ironic smile. "I didn't mean to answer."

"Couldn't help yourself?"

He was good at sidestepping personal questions, but he hadn't this time.

"Sometimes if you let things out, they have less power to hurt," she said.

Who's hurting? his macho inner voice

piped up, and he instantly shut it down. Pretending that his parents' lack of interest in him hadn't affected him was an exercise in futility. Of course it had bothered him, and it bothered him even more now that he had Livia. It made him wonder what he'd been lacking.

"I tried to make amends a few years after the showdown where they cut me off financially. Suddenly having no money was a shock, but I could accept their reasoning, and I didn't hold a grudge. I was of age, after all. A few years later, after my first really good rodeo season, I decided that maybe we could work things out. That maybe if I went at it logically, rather than emotionally, it would be okay."

What are you doing talking about this stuff?

But now that he'd started, it was like he couldn't stop.

"When I contacted my dad, he was certain—*so certain*—that I was crawling back asking for money. He began our conversation by gloating over my capitulation to the mighty dollar, and assuring me that life would be better if I toed the line in the future. I was twenty-two years old. Not exactly toe-the-line age, and I did not take that well."

"Especially since it you didn't intend to ask for money."

"Exactly. The blowup that followed was spectacular. We both said things I'd like to think we regret." He gave Kat a long look. "But some things, once said, are hard to let go of."

"What did he say?"

Troy hesitated, because his dad hadn't been the only one who'd lost his temper. Having gone home with the best of intentions and being met by an arrogant I-told-you-so attitude had hurt.

"It was something along the lines of I had always disappointed him. I can't remember the exact words." But he could remember the impact of them. It had been like a hammer to the chest. It was so unfair to have a parent who ignored you talk about disappointment. He could have raged back, made several justified points, but instead, he'd left in cold silence.

Cold silence pretty much described their relationship from that point on.

Kat set her hands in her lap as she shifted in the seat to look at him. "I can't imagine getting a message like that from my family."

"Not to be dramatic, but they aren't my family anymore. My family is waiting for me at Daisy Lane."

"Then I guess you'd better go get her."

He didn't know whether Kat noted the time or the fact that he needed to escape this conversation. His nerves were thrumming, as they tended to do before a bronc ride, or after discussing matters he never intended to discuss. Matters he'd prefer to avoid discussing in the future. He needed to make that clear.

"Right." He got out of the truck, and before closing the door, he said, "I'd rather not talk about this again. I like to leave the past in the past."

"I understand."

He wished he did, because no matter how many times he told himself that he was over it, the lingering sting of abandonment always stunned him. The fact that he'd shared kind of stunned him, too. His hard and fast rule about never speaking about his parents other than in the most superficial way had been broken.

It worried him.

Kat got out of the truck and indicated the barn with a jerk of her head. "I'm going to see about the feeders. See you later."

"See you." Troy headed toward his truck, trying to relax his taut muscles.

He wasn't giving in to hurt. He was moving on with his life and doing the sensible thing—avoiding situations that led to such pain. He'd meant it when he'd told Kat that he wouldn't allow himself to become dependent on people or things that disappeared. He'd had enough of that in his life.

Tiff, whom he'd loved even when it became evident that she couldn't love him back. Herm and Grace, who'd helped him with Livia. His career with the rodeo. Even his relationship with his parents. All gone.

He could live with losing his rodeo career—the injury had healed, but he had

Livia now and needed a stable career. Getting ground into the dirt didn't qualify.

As to the people, it was hard to admit that he'd needed them. With Herm and Grace, it had been a natural parting, sad but necessary, as they'd moved on with their lives. With Tiff and his parents…it had been a twist of the knife.

He wouldn't go through that again.

He wouldn't risk getting too close to Kat, mainly because he wanted to. That want, that desire for the anchor of family, of belonging, always seemed to blow up in his face.

Fortunately, Kat was on the same page, having been hurt by that jerk ex-boyfriend of hers. In an odd way, it was like having an ally.

But he was still going to watch himself and remember that his life was more predictable when it was just him and Livia.

IF TROY HAD shown up for work the next morning with sticky note on his jacket that read, "Superficial discussions only, please," the message would have been only slightly clearer than the one Kat was receiving as they stretched smooth wire between posts. Troy didn't want to talk, and when he did talk, it was about fencing. She did not take it personally. Well, not much anyway.

Troy had a shoeing job later that afternoon. He'd managed to book Livia into daycare for the job, but he'd insisted on the two of them coming out with Kat this morning. Now Livia played on a blanket laid over the meadow grass, and Troy was constantly swiveling to check on her. And he wasn't talkative.

Telling her about his family had hurt.

Did they know how their son felt?

What would it be like to have parents who ignored you? Kat had to admit that while she'd put a little distance between herself and the home ranch, it was the healthy kind of distance. If she needed anything, or her family needed anything, there was no question about needs being met. Her friends Maddie and Whit were the same. Tight families. Maddie's family had moved after she graduated high school, but Kat and Whit's family stepped in when she needed assistance.

No wonder Troy was such a solo act. When he'd said that thing about not becoming dependent on people and things that disappear…

Livia started crying, and Kat headed to the blanket to pick her up. Troy also started toward her, but seeing that Kat had the situation under control, he went back to ratcheting the fence stretcher.

Kat teased Livia out of her tears and propped the baby on a hip. She waded through the tall grass to where Troy was releasing the stretcher after hammering in the last of the staples. Livia started investigating Kat's hair, working her fingers through the curls, and when Troy reached for her, she shook her head.

"So it's like that, eh?" He smiled at his daughter, who waved her arms and gave a crow of delight before playfully burying her face in Kat's shoulder.

"We girls stick together," Kat said just before the baby twisted in her arms and made a dive for her dad, who caught her.

She was glad to see Troy engaging again, even if his gaze held a wary edge as it met hers. She'd done nothing to earn that wariness, so it had to have something to do with him busting loose with his story yesterday.

"You girls stick together?" Troy repeated, dipping his chin to smile into his baby daughter's eyes. His phone chirped in the pocket of the jacket he'd shed shortly after they'd started work. Kat picked up the jacket from the tailgate and held it while he dug the phone out of the pocket with his free hand. He read the screen and then tucked the phone into his back pocket.

"A friend of mine works for a special rodeo tour. She's trying to get me on board."

Kat's stomach twisted in an odd way. "Are you interested?"

"I'm out of shape. I have a kid. I have a job waiting for me."

"So that's a maybe?" Kat leaned back against the tailgate and folded her arms over her middle.

He grinned at her, the first crack in his distant facade all morning.

"Welcome back," she said softly.

He gave her a sheepish look. "Thanks," he muttered dryly.

"You know what?"

"What?"

She unfolded her arms and clasped the warm tailgate on either side of her thighs. "I don't want anything from you except for what you're already giving." She tilted her head toward the fence they were working on. "That's it. Yesterday, you let loose with some personal information. Today, you're clammed up like you're afraid I'll pry more out of you. You said you didn't want to discuss it, and I took you at your word."

"I'm not…" His mouth tightened as he regarded her from under the bill of his ball cap. "I am. Fine. I'll un-clam."

"I'm not going to pester you for details." She was actually kind of insulted that he would think she would… Except she had pestered him to accept help, so maybe he was slightly justified.

"It's not that I think you'll prod me for details—"

"It's that you said anything at all?"

He gave a slow nod. "Pretty much."

"I guess we both had a first." Kat pushed off the tailgate and moved toward him. "I have never before kissed someone just because I felt like it." Not something she would normally confess, but her relationship with Troy wasn't like any relationship she'd had. He was so emotionally wary that it made her feel bold.

It took him a few seconds to decide to engage. "Why not?"

The corners of her mouth tilted slightly. "Because I usually concoct long chains of possible consequences. In other words, I practice being the opposite of Andrew, James and Kent. But with you, I kissed first, thought about it later. And it didn't ruin my life or my independence." She leaned closer. "Huge breakthrough."

Livia held out her arms, and Kat automatically took her from Troy, whose hands fell away only after he was certain his daughter was secure in Kat's grasp.

"I look at consequences," he said. She raised an eyebrow in a skeptical expression, and he explained, "I might have jumped off cliffs, but I knew all the risks. I did my research."

"Then jumped anyway."

"Pretty much. But I don't live that way anymore. I'm not jumping, Kat."

Kat drew in the sweet scent of Livia's downy hair as the little girl squirmed against her. There was no mistaking Troy's meaning. They might be attracted to one another, but he wasn't taking any risks. Wasn't about to get involved with her in any kind of a serious way.

She was relieved that they were on the same page, but that didn't keep pride from taking command.

"You don't need to warn me off, Troy. I learned my lesson with Derek, and until I trust myself—"

"I wasn't warning you off."

She lifted her eyebrows because it had certain seemed like a warning. She drew in a breath and reiterated her position. "All I what is what you're offering. Help on the farm. Maybe a pleasant conversation. We don't need to swap secrets."

But as she studied the guy in front of

her—cowboy, helpmate, father—she had the unsettling feeling that she wasn't telling the entire truth. She was curious about his secrets, and yes…she felt tempted to share her own. But that was a slippery slope, and when she thought about sliding down it, her insides twisted.

"Kat," he said in a low voice that seemed to roll over her. "I'm warning myself off."

"Oh." Her cheeks began to feel warm.

"I'm not in a good place. I don't know if I ever will be. I'm attracted to you, but I can't be more than a friend." He drew in a breath as his gaze held hers. "Which works, because that's all you want, too, right?"

It was at that moment that Kat knew she was about to tell a lie.

"Right."

What she was beginning to want—something deeper, something more—didn't matter, because in Kat's estimation, sharing a strong friendship was so much better than losing oneself by falling in love.

CHAPTER TEN

PATRICIA KNOX ARRIVED with her five Arabians half an hour ahead of schedule. She unloaded each in turn, tying the horse to the trailer and then removing the protective leg coverings they wore.

"I hate it when they skin their legs up," she said as she tackled the last horse, a dancing bay gelding.

They released the animals into the corral and watched as the horses carefully explored their surroundings.

"I won't let them into the pastures until they spend a night in the smaller corral and get used to the sights and sounds." Kat turned to Patricia as she spoke.

"Great. I think they're going to be happy here. So much more room to run."

Kat showed Patricia the freshly cleaned tack room where she hung her halters, then they stepped out into the sun to watch the horses.

"They're beautiful," Kat said.

The Tennessee walkers were arriving tomorrow. Their owner had stopped by the previous evening and given Littlegate Farm their approval.

"Do you have a horse?" Patricia asked.

"Not yet. I'm still settling in. I haven't even fully unpacked." But Kat would have a horse eventually.

"I lived in my house for over a year before I hung pictures."

"Then you know what I'm talking about. Between the day job and getting the fences worked on, I haven't had much time for home organization."

"That's what winter is for, dear."

Her dad used to say the same thing.

"Is Troy off shoeing?"

"He is."

"He's a nice addition to the community," Patricia said on a wry note. "And that baby. What a doll."

"She is," Kat agreed. The ranch felt kind of lonely when Troy and Livia weren't here, but that was something she needed to get used to, because she was certain that Troy was moving to larger quarters as soon as he could.

Would they remain friends? Or just be nodding acquaintances who bumped into one another in the grocery store from time to time?

A poignant question she didn't want to think about.

"I wanted to ask Troy his thoughts concerning glue-on horseshoes, but maybe I can catch him tomorrow."

"Maybe," Kat agreed. She really didn't need to worry about her farm becoming a lonely place when Troy left. She'd have people coming and going to visit their horses. Patricia had already told her that she intended to come out several days a week.

"I haven't been in this area since I was a girl," Patricia said as they walked together to her truck.

"It is a little isolated." Littlegate Farm and the property beyond it formed an island of private land in the surrounding Forest Service land.

"Your aunt kept a very tidy property," Patricia continued. "I thought it looked like a fairy tale farm."

"Did you visit Littlegate Farm?"

"No. The hots springs." When Kat gave her a bemused look, Patricia explained, "There was a hot spring on the Bealman place, but it quit flowing maybe twenty years ago."

"I had no idea."

"Probably because you would have been—what? Six at the time?"

"Close."

"And the Bealmans liked to keep to themselves. Missy and I became best friends in kindergarten, though, so I got to visit and play in the warm water. It was heavenly. Mr. Bealman talked of starting some kind of healing waters resort or spa or something, but then there was an earthquake, and the spring stopped flowing."

Interesting.

"Are you still in contact with your friend?"

"No, unfortunately."

"I was just wondering if the Bealmans

were considering putting their place on the market." Because if they were, she had a good idea why Dane was interested in her place. The road to the Bealman place crossed her property, and it was not a county-maintained road. It was, in essence, Kat's road, to do with as she pleased. She wouldn't shut off access to a neighbor, but what if a potential buyer didn't want to depend on her goodwill?

"I haven't heard anything about that, and I'm sure such a thing would cause a buzz." Patricia lifted her eyebrows in a nod to the nature of small communities.

Kat understood her point, but what if there was a private deal with people willing to pay the price for anonymity. Tight lips were not the norm in the community, but what if a person had reason to keep things secret?

Maybe someone didn't want the price of a neighboring property to skyrocket before they had a chance to buy it for a song.

She might be edging into conspiracy theory territory, but even after Patricia had driven away and Kat was back at her computer entering numbers into a spreadsheet, she kept turning the idea over in her head.

When Troy got home late that afternoon, she shot him a text asking if he'd like a beer. As a friend, of course, but she didn't type out that part. He knocked on her door ten minutes later. Livia was in his arms, but her eyes were drooping.

"Too much excitement at daycare," he said as he stepped into the living room. "You've been busy."

"Yes. I moved all the boxes from here into the spare bedroom."

He smiled, and Kat's heart did the familiar micro stutter. She went to the fridge for the beer, and when she returned to the living room, she saw Troy had laid Livia on the sofa with a pillow at her side to keep her from rolling off. Livia showed zero interest in sleep, instead pinching the fabric between her tiny fingers and kicking her feet.

"I see Patricia's horses have settled in."

"She's coming back tomorrow, and I'm going to help her lead them around the pasture boundaries." A precaution to keep them from running through a fence they didn't know was there. "Then we'll turn them loose, and the corral will be free for the older mare coming later this week. She needs medication, so I'll keep her close to the house."

After Kat handed him the open beer, Troy sat on the floor with his back resting against the sofa close to where his daughter was sleeping. Kat perched on the chair.

"I'd like your opinion on something."

Troy gave her a polite look. There'd been a lot of polite looks since they'd discussed their mutual expectations and settled on friendship. She pulled the map she'd printed from the end table next to her and passed it to him.

"I outlined the Bealman property—the place up the road from Littlegate Farm—in blue and Littlegate Farm in green. All the rest is federal land."

"Okay."

"What do you see?"

"I see a green property in front of a blue property."

"Blocking access."

"Yes."

"Which may or may not be a thing. But… do you think it might be?"

Troy frowned as he studied the map. "That depends on a lot of factors."

"That's what I'm coming to understand. What if that's the reason Dane was so hot to get this place? Is it possible that having access to the Bealman property is a thing?"

"We could ask him."

Kat smiled and tipped the top of her beer in Troy's direction. "He'd love that, but I don't want to tip my hand."

Her expression sobered as she studied the wall behind the sofa. She'd come so close to sacrificing Littlegate Farm for Derek. So close to allowing him to bamboozle her into giving up the place to his brother. That stung.

It also changed your life.

She shifted her gaze to Troy, who was watching Livia run her fingers over the textured fabric of the pillow, making little scratchy sounds that she found highly entertaining.

Friends.

For how long?

She didn't want to think about it, and she didn't want to think about how lonely the farm was going to be after he left. The push and pull of wanting what she didn't want to want was starting to get to her.

As THE DAYS PASSED, Troy fell into a routine. One of the regulars at Daisy Lane Daycare was on a family holiday, and Troy was able to take advantage. Thanks to the need for farriers in the Larkspur Valley, he was booked fairly solid. He was going to have to say no more often after he started working full time, which meant that he'd have to decide what clients were an automatic yes.

Walt Stenson was one. He'd taken another trip to the old man's place to do follow-up work on the stud and trim two brood mares that were almost as cranky as the stud but not as lethal with their teeth. He couldn't help but wonder what kind of foals came out of such cranky parents, but he hadn't been in the area long enough to subtly suss out an answer. Questions as well as answers were repeated in small communities, and Troy erred on the side of caution in that regard.

He felt comfortable enough with Walt to ask him his opinion of Dane Cashman of Cashman Real Estate while he worked on the stud's feet.

Walt gave him a considering look. "Are you thinking of buying?"

"When the time is right, yes. I probably will." And he'd thought it sounded less personal if he included the name of the guy's business.

"You haven't talked to him yet?"

"No. I was just wondering about him. What he'd be like to work with."

"Funny, because he was asking about you."

Troy's chin came up. "We met when he stopped by Littlegate Farm to talk to Kat. Maybe he was wondering how she got a tenant so quickly."

"Maybe," Walt conceded. "He was asking about you in that kinda overly casual way he has when he's pumping people. His dad was the same way."

Troy set down the hoof and then stood,

taking a moment to stretch his back. "Did he get any information?"

Walt shook his head. "Nothing other than you're replacing Bobby at L&S in a few weeks."

"Not much else to know about me."

"Right…so why was he digging?"

Troy shook his head, moved as if to pick up Jack's nearside rear foot and then stopped. "Do you know of any plans for housing developments or anything like that in the area?"

"I don't." But Troy could tell the old man was curious. "Cashman asked about you, and you're asking about housing developments. What's going on?"

"Between you and me, I'm wondering if he has something in the works."

"A housing development?" Walt considered for a moment. "A few years ago, I would have said, 'Unlikely, because there's not enough work in the area.' But I guess with people making a living on their computer, it's possible."

Walt put a hand on his stud's hip, and the big horse cocked a leg, relaxing under the old man's touch. If Walt had been physically able to trim feet, Troy believed that the horse would have stood for him.

"If someone was looking at selling a big chunk of land, it would be a farmer or rancher, and I think word would have traveled." Walt patted the stud and put his hands into the pockets of his canvas jacket. "Do you want me to find out? Quiet-like?"

Troy regarded Walt. "You could do that? Quiet-like?"

"When you're an old coot who speaks his mind, people don't expect you to be subtle. It's not like I have my finger on the pulse of the community, but I do meet the boys for coffee in the mornings."

Meaning he had his finger on the pulse of the community. Troy had spent enough of his off-season on ranches to know how much agricultural people loved to talk. Something about spending long hours alone driving in circles, he imagined.

Troy studied Jack's hoof, picked it back up and started to rasp. The horse laid his ears back. "Here now," Walt said, and the big horse dropped his nose, indicating he'd put up with this nonsense a while longer.

Troy ran his gaze over the stud, who flattened his ears again and then looked back at Walt.

"Do not comment on the resemblance," the old man grumbled. Troy gave an appreciative smile, even as part of him wondered if this was this his future, being an old guy living alone, waiting for his daughter to call.

"Wouldn't dream of it."

"You going to tell me what's going on?"

"After I figure out a few things, yes."

"Does it involve Margo Stokes's farm?" Troy didn't answer, and Walt gave a nod. "We'll talk after you figure a few things out."

Troy packed his tools and started down Walt's twisty driveway when his phone rang. Kat.

"Hi."

"When you finish, would you be able to pick me up at my parents' ranch? I had… car trouble."

"Sure. I'm on my way to pick up Livia now."

"I'd appreciate it."

There was something in her tone that made him ask, "Is everything all right?"

"It's…normal," she said. "The ranch is easy to find. After you leave Larkspur going north, take Glen Mill Road, which is the first right off the highway. Keep following it until it forks. Go left, then continue on until you see the Farley Ranch sign on the gate."

"Will do."

"No hurry. I just need a ride home before nightfall."

Troy didn't know what to expect when he approached the Farley Ranch twenty minutes later, but the festive floral wreath decorating the main gate surprised him.

He'd gathered from Kat that her mother was an artist, and he knew that James was a guy who wrestled steers as a hobby. Other than that… Well, he knew nothing, and he was curious about Kat's family. She talked about trying to control the wild schemes her brothers came up with, so he'd half expected a rundown property. Instead, he drove into a neatly maintained operation.

The ranch was set up in a classic manner with a barn, two metal grain silos, a few out buildings, a machine shed and wooden corrals. There was also the classic farm junkyard to one side, with old tractors, balers and various pieces of outdated farm equipment slowly deteriorating in the wind, rain and snow. But all in all, it was a nice-looking place.

He couldn't help but give the barn a second glance as he walked by with Livia in his arms. From the stories Kat told, it sounded as if her brothers spent more time on the roof than off it, but there wasn't a single Farley to be seen on the edifice today.

He stopped dead when he saw Kat's gray Toyota Camry. Something had destroyed the windshield. He moved closer and gave a choked laugh when he saw pieces of green pumpkin embedded in what was left of the shattered glass and spread across the front seat.

"Welcome to my world."

Troy turned to see Kat standing at the gate to the front yard.

"How?"

"My brother Kent is home for a bit, and he's determined to win a pumpkin chunking contest when he heads back to Wyoming for the Labor Day celebrations. This is the result of the practice run."

Livia held out her arms to Kat, who reached over the gate to take her. She propped his baby on her hip like a pro, and Troy found himself torn between admiration at her casual technique and concern at how attached Livia was getting to Kat. Judging from the way Kat was grinning at his daughter as she tickled a foot, the affection went both ways.

No big deal.

Say it enough times, and you'll believe it.

Fine. No big deal.

He forced a carefree smile on his face and assured himself he wasn't getting in too deep, despite noting the way the sunlight glinted off Kat's hair as she cooed at Livia or that the curve of her cheek fascinated him.

No. Not too deep. He had this under control. He wasn't risking yet another loss.

"Thank you for coming," she said, handing the baby back to Troy after he came through the gate she'd opened. "James and Kent are out looking for a replacement windshield. They would run me home when they get back, but sometimes getting back can be an issue."

The door opened behind Kat, and an older version of her stepped onto the small porch.

"Hi," the woman said warmly. "I'm Emily Farley. It's nice to meet you finally."

"Mom, this is Troy Mackay and Livia."

Emily Farley made a beeline for the baby, and when she reached for her, Livia didn't duck for cover as usual. Instead, she seemed fascinated by the long fringed western earrings Emily wore. Obviously a baby pro, Kat's mom popped off the earrings as soon as Livia batted at them and tucked them into her jeans pocket.

"Will you stay for dinner?" she asked. "I was just about to put it on the table."

Troy glanced at Kat, who gave him a

Your choice look in response. If he was going to be part of this community, he should get to know the people.

"Sure, if it's not a bother."

She waved a hand. "Never a bother setting an extra plate at the table." She handed Livia back to him. "And since I may not see my sons anytime soon, I'd like to have someone enjoy my mac and cheese fresh out of the oven.

Kat moved closer to Troy as her mom disappeared into the house. "Do me a favor? Don't mention Dane Cashman to my family. They get protective."

She wanted to handle things alone. He understood.

"I'll keep my mouth shut."

Kind of a specialty of his.

KAT HADN'T EXPECTED to stay for dinner, but if Troy didn't mind—and he didn't seem to—then she wasn't going to turn down her mom's homemade macaroni and cheese. Try as she might, she was never quite able to duplicate the recipe.

She held Livia while Troy helped her

mom put dinner on the table. He knew his manners, pitched in when he could and respected her mom's wishes when she shooed him away. And as she watched him setting the table, Kat sensed that he enjoyed the small task.

Could it be that Troy Mackay, cliff jumper and bronc rider, was a secret homebody? All signs pointed to yes.

"I wish my husband was here so that you two could meet," Emily said after setting the casserole on the table, "but he and Andrew are on a buying trip."

"Cattle?" Troy asked.

"I wish," Emily said softly. Then she smiled. "Old tractor."

"As if we don't have enough of them lying around," Kat said.

"Special tractor," Emily clarified. "Jubilee edition of the Ford N."

The dogs started barking, and Emily leaned toward the window. "I guess the two extra plates are going to come into use," she said as James's truck pulled up beside Troy's.

Kat's brothers dropped to the ground

from either side of the truck, shut the doors and headed to the house.

"Just in time," Emily called as they came through the door. "Wash up."

"Did you find a windshield?" Kat asked a few minutes later when, after greeting Troy, they took seats at the table.

"We decided to go with a new one," Kent said as he scooped up a healthy portion of mac and cheese and plopped it onto his plate next to the green beans with bacon. "Safety and all that."

"Couldn't find one at the salvage yard?"

"Actually, we did. But we decided that for our only sister, we want the best."

"I appreciate it," she said.

Livia, seated on Troy's lap, leaned over her father's arm in an attempt to reach for Kent's plate. Her brother seemed uncertain as to how to defend himself from a determined baby. Finally, he handed her a bean, which she took, examined closely and then smacked her dad in the face with it.

"Sorry, man," Kent said in a startled voice. "I didn't realize she'd weaponize it."

"I'm used to it," Troy said. "Carrots are worse."

"You guys are off the hook for the art show," Emily said to Kent and James. "Kat's going to help."

"Thank you," Kent said to Kat before shooting a look at their mom. "Not that I don't enjoy hanging artwork in the gallery."

"I know," Emily replied patiently. "But one of you is going to help me haul grandma's furniture to Kat's house tomorrow. Early."

Kent and James exchanged glances. "Andrew."

Emily rolled her eyes while Kat wondered what she was going to do with the furniture stored in the shed next to the barn. Yes, she needed a few pieces, but this was an all-or-nothing deal. Kat went with all.

They finished eating, and after clearing the table, Kent said to no one in particular, "Want to go dial in the pumpkin chunker?"

The beastly piece of primitive machinery that had fired a green pumpkin into her windshield? Kat thought not.

She shook her head. "I've had enough of the chunker today." She turned to Troy. "If you'd like to give it a try. I'll watch Livia."

She could see the battle going on in Troy's head. On the one hand, he was all about doing his duty, watching his daughter, helping with post dinner chores, getting Kat home. On the other…projectiles fired from a homemade cannon.

"Go," Kat said.

He grinned at her. "All right. I will."

CHAPTER ELEVEN

CHUNKING PUMPKINS WAS ridiculously cathartic. After several shots, Troy and Kat's brothers had the sights dialed in, and the green pumpkins were hitting the scarecrow target every time. No one was interested in stopping until the very last pumpkin had been fired, and Kent declared himself satisfied.

"Distance and accuracy," he said. "I'm going to bring home that prize money."

"And all it will cost is a couple hundred bucks for a new windshield," James said.

Kent sucked a breath through his teeth. "That's definitely going to cut into the prize money, but I'll still have bragging rights." He rolled the cannon into the shop. "Want a beer?"

"Sure." Troy replied. Kat and her mom were busy in the house, and Livia was with them, so he had two hands to drink with for a change.

Kent went to the mini fridge, pulled out two beers, tossed one to James and the other to Troy. James didn't hesitate to pop the cap, allowing foam to spew over the top and onto the concrete. Troy opened his more cautiously, but there was no escaping the pressure buildup created by the toss-and-catch technique of beer delivery. Neither brother seemed to mind.

"I'm glad you're on the farm with Kat," James said as the three of them settled in the webbed lawn chairs near the open door of the shop. "Not to be the overprotective brother, but I worry about her living alone." He regarded his beer for a moment. "I might talk to her about getting another renter after you move out. We'd feel better with someone there."

Troy smiled a little, and James said, "What?"

"The way your family watches out for one another."

James shifted his gaze toward the house across the driveway as if making certain that no one had snuck up on them. "Kat hates being taken care of. As the oldest, she saw it as her job to take care of us, and she gets ticked when we do the same."

"We had to keep a lot of stuff secret," Kent added. "Otherwise, she would have had an ulcer by the time she was sixteen."

"Fourteen," James said. "Kat takes on stuff. Makes herself responsible for things that she's not responsible for."

Kent's forehead wrinkled. "We called her 'the sheriff.'"

"Do you still keep things from her?" Troy asked.

The brothers answered by exchanging looks.

"Not much anymore." Kent shook his head. "Now that we're not living under the same roof, it's different."

Troy wondered about that.

"She's eased up," James said.

"Yeah?" Troy was curious as to James's take on his older sister easing up.

"Kat built herself a pretty rigid life. I think she thought it was what she wanted, but she got impatient with it." He spoke with authority.

"Impatient?" Troy was openly curious.

James nodded. "There were little signs. She spent more time here when she visited, almost like she wanted to get away from the stick-in-the-mud boyfriend of hers."

"Derek's not a bad guy," Kent said, "but he's not right for Kat, and I was glad when they broke up. He worries about what message his tie sends."

James pointed a finger at Kent. "Don't wear stripes on stripes. Or do. I can't recall. Purple is bad."

"He's better than his brother," Kent said to Troy. "I would have hated having Dane Cashman as a brother-in-law."

"I don't think the brother of a brother-in-law is also a brother-in-law," James said.

Kent sent his brother a scowling look. "I would have had to tolerate him, and most of the time, I just want to punch him out."

"He sells real estate?" Troy had promised not to discuss Dane Cashman with Kat's brothers, but since they'd brought it up, he saw no harm in gathering some intel.

"He handles a lot of high-end clients. The people who don't want you to know that they bought a seven-thousand-square-foot—" James made air quotes "—*summer home* in the area. Like we don't notice the private jets landing at the airport."

"Dane speaks their language," Kent said.

"Private school," James added. "Larkspur High was good enough for his brother but not good enough for him. He left after his freshman year, I think."

"But he came back," Troy pointed out.

"Big fish. Small pond."

"Ah." That actually made sense.

"He has clout in the community, and a lot of people like him and his family, who donate to worthy causes," Kent said.

"He wouldn't have much luck as a salesman if people didn't like him," James added.

Troy didn't like him.

"Are you guys done destroying things?" Kat called as she started across the driveway from the front gate of the house. She had Livia on her hip, and when the little girl spotted Troy, she started making impatient noises. Troy got out of his chair as she approached and took Livia.

"Time to go?" he asked Kat, thinking it was a good guess, since Livia was wearing her coat and sunhat.

"It's time." Livia took hold of a hank of Kat's hair as she spoke, and Kat patiently pried the little girl's fingers off her curls. "I might invest in a swim cap."

"I can cut it short for you," James said.

She gave her brother a dark look. "Thank you, no. Once was enough." When Troy met her gaze with a questioning look, she said, "I was asleep. Long story."

"Seems to be a lot of those on this ranch," he said in a low voice and was rewarded with a smiling glance. He was becoming addicted to smiling glances, and he needed to get a grip.

"So, guys, stay out of trouble," Kat said. "I can expect my car back..."

Kent met James's gaze. "Three days?"

"Make it two. And I want it fixed right."

"Two days," Kent said. "Fixed right."

"Delivered?"

"Yes."

"No pumpkin residue?"

"None."

"Good." She turned to Troy. "I'm ready to go."

It was so natural to put his hand on the small of her back as they walked to the truck. Troy didn't know he'd done it until his fingers touched the fabric of her shirt. Kat's shoulder bumped his as his hand fell away, and Livia made a happy fan-girl squeal as she reached out to pat Kat's hair. It felt like they were a family or something.

Okay...maybe he was wading into waters he'd intended to stay out of. And he was going to have to think on that.

"LOOK AT THAT," Kat said, pointing at the fledgling owlets on the roof of her house. They bobbed and shuffled next to one another, taking turns stretching their wings. As Troy pulled to a stop near his trailer, one of the baby owls took to the air, awkwardly landing on the lower branches of the pine tree next to the barn. His or her siblings followed, the branches bouncing and bending as they landed.

"I wonder where the mother is," Troy said and got out of the truck.

"Probably waiting in the attic to scratch my eyes out." Kat got out of the truck and stood near the front bumper, watching the babies watch her. "There she is." She pointed to the Douglas fir next to the pine where the babies were once again testing their wings. There was definitely one adult owl in the thick branches, maybe two.

"I should be able to board up the hole in the vent in a week or two," Kat said. "There's no reason they can't live in the barn and keep the mice down."

She'd asked her mom about feral cats, but for once, the Farley Ranch had no mama cats, and Emily knew of no rescues. Owls would do the trick.

"Balance of life," she said as Troy lifted Livia out of the car seat. "Green pumpkin through the windshield, bad surprise. Owlets on the roof, good surprise."

"Do you think it works that way?"

"Today it does."

Troy had been quiet on the drive home, but he wasn't the most talkative guy under the best of circumstances. He met her eyes and smiled, and she could see that there were things going on in his head.

"I hope my family wasn't too much."

"You're lucky to have them." He started toward the camp trailer, and Kat fell into step with him.

"I know. They drive me a little crazy sometimes, but I am fortunate." And she didn't want to rub it in that Troy had the opposite kind of family situation. She still didn't understand, but she felt for him.

"You are." He stopped at the corner of the trailer, looked as if he wanted to say something and then changed his mind. There was the feel of a storm in the air, and Troy probably wanted to get his baby inside, but he didn't move.

"Is everything all right?"

He nodded, but she didn't believe him.

"Then I guess I'll see you tomorrow." She turned without waiting for a reply and strode across the driveway toward her dark house.

"Kat. Hang on."

She turned back, and Troy opened the

trailer door and set the baby carrier inside. Livia gave a happy coo, and Troy left the door open and came to meet Kat at the corner of the trailer. The wind swirled around them, picked up fir needles and bits of debris and then settled again.

She studied his face, wondering if he'd gotten some bad news. "If there is something wrong, you know we've got your back. My family and I."

He let out a breath, took her face between his hands, leaned down and kissed her. It was the first kiss they'd shared since repairing the fence, and it was different. There was a message in this kiss, coupled with a feeling of desperation. Or maybe it was simply a need for one another.

Kat wasn't thinking clearly enough to analyze it. She wound her arms around his neck and answered his desperation with some of her own. Her knees felt wobbly by the time Troy lifted his head, and her hands slid down the front of his jacket, coming to rest with her palms flat against his chest.

He brushed the curls away from her temple and brought his forehead down to touch hers. "Kat…"

His voice trailed, then he lifted his forehead from hers and looked at her in a way that told her he wasn't going to finish the thought. He might not even know how to finish it. And she wasn't sure she was ready to hear what he had to say, because the warm feeling that lingered after the kiss was starting to morph into something closer to alarm. If he did have a shift in his feelings, if he made a declaration, she'd have to decide what risks she was willing to take. Her gut said zero. She hadn't had enough time to recover from Derek's duplicity. Wasn't about to put a man's needs ahead of her own.

She didn't want to take any risks with her heart and her freedom.

Livia let out a squeal, shattering the silence, and Troy glanced toward the truck and then back at Kat.

She nodded, even though she wasn't clear on what she was agreeing to, then she turned and headed toward her house. The wind whipped at her jacket, and behind her, she heard Troy close the trailer door. She put her head down and hurried to her gate, not quite clear on whether she was trying to outrun the wind or distract herself from the unsettling thought that her summer cowboy was starting to feel like a very necessary part of her life.

THIS CAN'T CONTINUE.

Troy heated Livia's bottle, changed her, sat on the bench seat near the portable crib and fed her. His little girl patted the bottle as she ate, her blue gaze holding his, and he realized he was smiling despite the turmoil of his thoughts.

He could talk friendship all he wanted, but the truth was that he was falling in love with Kat Farley, and he had to come up with a way to handle the situation before he did something stupid. Like tell her when he wasn't ready to follow through.

He probably already had told her. The kiss they'd just shared, which had not been in his game plan, had felt different from the casual kisses they'd shared before, more of a statement than an exploration. The thought of setting himself up for another loss made him feel a little sick inside.

Kat takes on stuff.

James's words echoed through his head. Kat was generous and caring and concerned about those she loved. She might have left Larkspur to escape her rambunctious family and build a predictable life, but it hadn't taken. She was back, and even though she spoke of not concerning herself with her family's escapades, he was certain that she'd be the first one there if anyone needed assistance. She'd given him and Livia a place to live because she took on stuff, but she'd made clear what she wanted from him. Help on the farm. Friendly conversation.

Boundaries.

He needed to keep to them.

His focus needed to be on finding a place to live and settling into his new job. He also needed to convince Sass that he was happy with his new path. Although that wasn't such an issue, because after a final push, she'd let the matter lie.

When his phone rang shortly after he'd

lain Livia down, he found himself hoping it was Sass. Not so that she could nag him into going on tour but because he wanted to hear a friendly voice belonging to someone he wasn't falling in love with.

The caller wasn't Sass. It was a friend of Walt Stenson calling to see about getting shoes reset on her two mares. Benny La-Salle lived a good distance from Larkspur and wanted to know if he was interested.

Anything that put money in the coffers interested him, so he assured Benny that he was, and that since Livia was booked for Daisy Lane the next day, he could do it tomorrow. Benny agreed, and after getting directions to her place, Troy hung up, thinking that if nothing else, the farrier side gig was going as well as Arlie Stokes had promised him it would.

His future was still shaky, though, and he wasn't going to relax until he had good money in the bank and a place to live with normal sized appliances. Stepping into the unknown had been easy when it had been just him. But if he made a mistake now, he wasn't the only one affected.

Sobering thought, that. One that followed him to bed and made it difficult to sleep as the wind rocked the trailer.

Things will be okay. You're just so used to being slapped backward that it's hard to believe it won't happen again.

On that thought, he finally fell asleep.

BENNY, WHO WAS close to Walt's age, lived in a little homestead house tucked in a little mountain valley. She told Troy if he got onto the correct road—*which, by the way is unmaintained, but pretty good this time of year*—there was no way he could miss the place. That had been correct, since the road ended at the gate. More than once, Troy had convinced himself that he was on the wrong road, that he'd driven too far, and that he needed to go back. Then he topped a hill and saw the house and barn sitting in a picturesque meadow.

The job went well. Benny stayed while he reset shoes and talked his ear off. After he finished the second horse and tucked the payment into his shirt pocket, she invited him in for coffee, but he declined.

"My little girl is in daycare, and I'm supposed to pick her up by five."

"Then you'd best get going," Benny said. "Next time, bring her. Walt says she's real cute."

"I might," Troy said. He thanked the woman for calling him and started the long drive back to Larkspur. He'd timed himself driving in, and if all went well, he'd be back in Larkspur with a good thirty minutes to spare. He might be able to hit the grocery store alone. Not that he minded taking Livia; it was simply a lot faster when he was alone.

He was several miles from Benny's place when a call came in. The phone stuttered as it rang, telling him that he was barely in the service area, but he answered anyway.

"Troy? This is Louise from L&S."

Instant bad feeling. "Hi, Louise."

"Hon, I really hate to do this over the phone, but I think you should know…" Louise's voice fizzled out. Troy said hello a couple of times and then she was back. "Are you there?"

"I just drove through a dead zone." And was probably approaching another.

"Bobby isn't going to retire. His condition is such that he needs to keep his insurance until he goes on Medicare, and we can't leave you hanging until he's free to leave. I'm afraid we have to rescind our offer."

Troy went over a bump that tossed the truck sideways, but he barely noticed.

"I understand." He pushed the words out of his throat without letting his disappointment show. These things happen. After leading a charmed life for years and years, disappointments seemed to be happening to him with alarming frequency. First, the Michaels's surprise buyout, followed by Arlie cheating him, and now the job he thought he had nailed down was no more. It was almost as if the universe was sending him a message—your elbow is healed. Go back to rodeo.

"I know some people who are hiring," Louise said. "I can give you names. And, of course, if you're still interested when

Bobby does retire, we'd welcome you on-board."

"Thanks," Troy said. "I…might have another opportunity waiting for me."

"I'm so glad to hear that." The relief in Louise's voice was palpable. "And there's your horseshoeing, too."

"There's that," he agreed, but the clients would soon taper off until spring. "I'll let you know if I need those names."

The phone signal fizzed out again. He said hello and then got the multiple beeps that indicated the call had been dropped.

Troy leaned his head against the headrest and contemplated the inevitability of his next steps. He leaned forward to take a tighter grip on the steering wheel as he approached another set of ruts and washboards.

He would contact Sass, hope that she still had an opening on the tour. If so, he and Livia would hit the road, and he would ride horses that had earned reputations as unrideable broncs. He'd get beat up, but he'd make very good money. Even if he got injured, he was guaranteed a base salary for the tour. If he didn't get injured, he'd get bonuses for every successful ride.

If he got injured, who would take care of Livia? She'd been the reason behind the sane choices he'd been trying to make, but it seemed like he was getting pushed back to rodeo no matter what path he tried to take.

Maybe there was a reason for that.

One tour would give him enough money to make a decent start, then he'd find a nine-to-five job. Somewhere.

He reached for his phone and tried to dial Sass one-handed, but he couldn't get the phone to unlock. He finagled it to take his thumbprint and glanced up in time to see a bull moose with a massive rack covered in velvet step into the road in front of him. He let go of the phone and swerved. The phone hit the passenger door after flying out of his hand. The truck bumped over the berm and came to rest in the marshy bog next to the road.

Troy released his death grip on the steering wheel as the moose waded through the quagmire and stopped directly in front of the truck, quite possibly to mock him. A second later, the animal pushed on through the bog and disappeared into the trees.

Once the moose had disappeared, Troy leaned down to pick up his phone from the floor. No service. He tucked the useless phone into his pocket and got out of the truck to examine the damage, sinking to his ankles in marsh water. Not cool.

He made his way to the road, his feet suctioning into the mud the first few steps before he finally hit dry ground. He looked first toward Benny's place, then in the direction he was heading. He had a better chance of getting a cell signal going toward Larkspur, he decided.

This is two, his little voice whispered.

Troy didn't believe that bad things happened in threes, but if they did, he kind of wished the third thing would happen soon so he could start dealing with it.

CHAPTER TWELVE

THE BIG HORSE trailer with Farley written down the side pulled up to Kat's house at the promised time. As Kat came out of the house, Andrew got out of the passenger door to guide his mother as she backed the trailer to the front gate.

"Uh…" Kat hurried her steps. "I was thinking we could store this stuff in the barn until I…have room cleared for it." Kat wanted to look at the stuff before hauling it into her house in case she didn't want some of it and ended up having to haul it out again.

Andrew waved his hands, and Emily caught sight of him in the rearview mirror and stopped.

"Kat wants to check it out before she lets the stuff into her house," he called through cupped hands in order to be heard over the diesel engine. "Take it to the barn." Andrew gave his sister a knowing grin before following the trailer as it moved forward.

"It's probably dusty," Kat said, catching up with him.

"And moth-eaten and out of date, and we're so happy to have it out of the shed. It frees up a ton of space, you know."

"What will you store in all that freed-up space?" Kat asked as she wondered what she was going to do with the furniture.

"Don't you be worrying about that," Andrew said. "The question is, what are you going to do with this stuff?"

"Save it for you?"

"I'm never leaving home, so nice try."

"No other place would have you, so I guess that's just as well."

Andrew made a face at her, and Kat smiled. It felt good to be fourteen again, arguing with her twelve-year-old brother.

"There's nothing wrong with a guy living with his parents," Andrew said in an overly serious voice.

"Well, you're not in the basement. I'll give you that."

He reached out to tap her nose, which

had infuriated her back in the day. Now it just made her feel glad to be close to family again. Andrew did live on the ranch, as did James, but not in the family home. In typical Farley fashion, Andrew had found a singlewide mobile home on a nearby property that was free for the hauling and twice as big as the camp trailer he'd lent to Troy. He'd spent the winter gutting and rebuilding the interior. The last time Kat had taken a tour, she'd been impressed with the renovation. Her brother might have bad luck with fire and heights, but he was talented with a hammer.

"How's the new house?"

"It hasn't caught on fire yet."

"Probably because Mom hid all the matches."

"She hid the scissors, too, so no blood."

Kat cuffed her brother's shoulder, and he took a dancing step back before turning to wave their mother to a stop a few feet away from the barn door.

"Good thing I remembered to do that," he said as Kat rolled her eyes. "Hey, I saw your windshield. For safety's sake, you should watch where you park when you visit the ranch."

"For safety's sake, I might not visit for a while."

"Ah, come on. Isn't safety what we're all about on the Farley Ranch?" Andrew teased.

"Oh yes," Emily said as she joined Kat and Andrew. "I heard that we're on the short list for the Larkspur Safety Award."

If there was such an award, Kat knew for a fact that her family would not be in the running.

"They must not have heard about Dad and the roof," Andrew said.

"What about Dad and the roof?" Kat asked in alarm before she caught herself. If it had been serious, she would have heard.

"He's messing with you," Emily said. "If anyone is going to fall off the roof, it's this one." She patted her son's chest and turned to the trailer. "You may not be able to use all the pieces, but I hope you can work some of them in."

"I'm sure I can, Mom."

Kat hadn't seen her grandmother's furniture in a long time, but considering the fact that it'd been stored in a shed for at least four years, it was in good shape. And very, very 2000s. Turquoise and brown upholstery with tan motifs.

"A good vacuuming, and this will do nicely," she said, patting the love seat. The sofa was too big for the space, but she could use a lot of the other pieces—end tables, nightstands and bookcases.

"Anything you don't want, feel free to dispose of."

Kat could tell by her mom's tone that she meant it. She simply didn't want to be the person who handled the job.

"I'll find good homes for whatever I don't keep," she promised.

"Where is Troy," Emily asked, looking around the empty driveway. "I wanted Andrew to meet the baby."

"Resetting some shoes for some friend of Walt Stenson." She'd seen him briefly that morning as he'd carried Livia to the truck. He'd been in a hurry and hadn't given her more details.

"Sorry to have missed him." Emily

opened the truck door and said, "I almost forgot." She reached inside, slid an animal carrier across the seat and handed it to Kat. The carrier was heavier on one end than the other, and Kat adjusted her grip as a chorus of meows rose from the interior.

"I…"

"Barn cats," Emily said with a smile. "Three. Twelve weeks old."

"Are they tame?"

"Oh, heavens no. What good is a tame barn cat?"

"Good point."

"I got them from the vet's office this morning. Someone abandoned a litter on their doorstep last week. They're neutered and ready to hunt. Just keep them locked in the barn for a few days."

"Well…" Kat lifted the carrier. "Thanks, Mom."

Emily waved away the thanks and got into the truck while Andrew unloaded a huge bag of cat food from the back seat and set it inside the barn before rolling the big door closed.

"The rest of the litter came home with

us," he told her. "You know Mom and her rescues."

That she did. And she was glad that it was kittens this time, instead of peafowl, or llamas, or any of the other creatures that Emily had hauled to the home ranch over the years.

She waved as her mom and brother drove away and then lifted the carrier so that she could peer through the metal bars at the three gray tabbies huddled into a furry mass in the back.

"Welcome to Littlegate Farm," she murmured.

The population of which was growing by the day. Five Arabians, two Tennessee walkers, cats, cowboy, baby.

She started for the house, stopping in the middle of the driveway when her phone rang. It was a local number she didn't recognize, so she answered and found herself speaking to Daisy at Daisy Lane Daycare.

"Mr. Mackay gave us this number as an emergency contact."

"Has there been an emergency?" Kat asked on a gasp.

"No. But we're closing soon, and Mr. Mackey was supposed to be here fifteen minutes ago."

"Okay." Kat pushed her hair back. "Will I be able to pick up Livia?"

"Your name is here for pickups."

"Great. I'm sure he just ran into some trouble on the job. I'll be right there."

And she'd be driving the old fencing truck. Drat Kent and his pumpkin chunking. She hurried to her house to get keys and a coat. On the way, she found Walt Stenson's phone number and called him. No answer. That would have been too easy.

Keys and coat in hand, she crossed the drive to the camp trailer and opened the door. Troy kept a neat home. Thankfully, his calendar was on the counter next to a small rack of clean dishes. She flipped the pages, hoping that he'd written down the client's name.

Sure enough. Benny LaSalle was written down on today's date for one o'clock. Benny lived at the very end of Halfmoon Road. Unless Troy had encountered some difficulties coming home, he should have been back by now.

Did she call the sheriff or just let this play out for a while?

By the time she got the old Ford started, she had her plan. She would pick up Livia, maybe drop her at Maddie's store since she didn't have a car seat, and then head out and see if she could find Troy. He wasn't answering his phone, but she wasn't surprised because of where Benny LaSalle lived. If he'd had engine trouble, he was probably walking and would eventually get a cell signal. In the meantime, she would keep calling.

Her gut was in a knot, but the calm of battle kept her from dwelling on it. This was a replay of a zillion episodes in her past.

Except this one concerned Troy, and it felt different.

TWO RAVENS FLEW tree to tree, shadowing Troy as he walked down the road holding up his phone every hundred yards or so to check for a signal. Livia was in a safe place, and although he felt bad about not being there at the promised time, he was more concerned about Kat worrying about where he was if they called her. She didn't have a car, so it wasn't like she could go looking for him. She could call her brothers. At this point, Troy wasn't concerned about being a burden to people he didn't know that well. He'd take a rescue if it got him to his daughter.

At least the weather was good. The sun shone with just enough warmth to counteract the crisp breeze, and though the road was wet from the previous night's rain, it was sand-based and not slippery. Birds called from the trees, and he spooked a couple of whitetail deer bedded down in an aspen grove as he rounded a corner.

Had he not had somewhere to be, it might have been a pleasant walk. But he did have a destination.

The ravens were the first to alert him to the approaching vehicle. He couldn't hear it over the winds, but he caught sight of the truck traveling the road a couple miles below him before it disappeared into a stand of trees.

It wasn't long before he heard the sound of an engine working as it propelled the rig along the road. He stopped walking, waiting near the edge of the road, and when the one-ton truck came into sight, he noted a familiar figure at the wheel. Kat had managed to find him.

Of course, she had. This was Kat's forte.

As she pulled up beside him, he was relieved to see Livia in a rear-facing car seat.

"Hey," Kat said, leaning an arm on the open window frame. "What happened?"

"I almost hit a moose." He went to the passenger side of the truck and opened the door. When he settled into the seat next to his daughter, she squealed and waved her arms at him.

"Hi, Button. Did you have a good day?" He tickled her chin, and she blew a raspberry at him before he met Kat's gaze over the car seat.

"Daisy had a seat to loan. I told her I'd drop it off tomorrow." She stepped on the clutch as she spoke and wrestled the gear-shift into second. "Where's your truck?"

"In a bog a couple miles up the road."

"Think we can pull it out? I have chains in the back."

"I think we can."

Kat let out the clutch, and the truck lurched forward. It was a heavy beast, tightly sprung, and the ride was not a comfortable one, but Livia seemed to enjoy the bumping and rocking. She smiled a drooly grin as Troy gave her his finger to grab.

"I didn't know this thing could make it this far."

"Neither did I, but it was my only choice after Daisy called and told me you were MIA. I checked your calendar, and that's how I knew where to find you." She smiled a little. "Sorry about trespassing."

"I appreciate it, Kat." He smiled, and from the way her eyebrows drew together into a faint frown, he knew that he hadn't managed to hide the heavy stuff he was dealing with. Like no job. Or rather having to take a job that he'd never intended to—if it was still available. If not...

You'll come up with something.

He had to. For Livia's sake.

"There it is," he said as Kat rounded a corner and started down the hill to the boggy bottom. The rear wheels of the truck were still on solid ground, so he was confident that they could pull it out of the quagmire.

"This is the best that you could do?" Kat said as she pulled to a stop just past the truck. "My brothers would have had both axles buried."

"I didn't realize the bar was so high," he murmured.

"Try harder next time." Kat gave him a quick look, as if trying to figure out what was on his mind, then she opened her door and dropped to the ground.

"Stay put," he said to Livia, who made a protesting noise. "We'll be quick." He hoped.

They were quick. Kat knew exactly what to do, which put her a step ahead of him, who'd never pulled a truck out of a bog before. She directed him as he attached the chains, and then he got into the driver's seat of the one-ton and started pulling his truck free.

"You're good with a clutch," she said after the truck had been dragged back onto the road. He gave her a look, and she blushed a little. "Truck driver. Right."

Actually no. He was not a truck driver, but they would talk about that later. After he called Sass and found out where he stood.

Livia was yelling from the front seat of Liv's truck but quieted when Troy transferred her to his. "We'll be home soon, and you can eat," he assured her. She'd probably fall asleep as soon as he started driving, which would allow him time to call Sass and hatch some kind of a plan.

"See you at the farm?" he said to Kat through the open window of his muddy truck, taking care to keep all stress out of his voice.

Kat's expression told him she knew something was up, but she simply said, "Yes. See you there."

WHAT HAD HAPPENED to Troy since the last time she saw him? Kat glanced into the rearview mirror as if seeing his truck could somehow crack the mystery.

Getting stuck in a bog while avoiding a moose would put anyone into a bad frame of mind. Kat didn't think that was behind Troy's mood, though, which was very reminiscent of the first night that they'd met. He was stressed, maybe a touch desperate, almost as if he'd been hit by some new obstacle.

What?

None of your business, unless he cares to share.

The answer, while true, didn't satisfy her.

She hadn't intended for things to get to the point where Troy Mackay was the first thing she thought of when waking up in the morning and the last she thought of before going to sleep. She'd honestly believed that since they were both coming out of failed relationships—both starting down new life paths that required their full attention—that, exploratory kisses aside, they could maintain a casual friendship.

That had been the plan.

It might not have worked.

After they got back to Littlegate Farm, Kat parked the one-ton truck behind the barn. When she came back around the building, Troy was lifting Livia out of his truck. Kat almost went to the house, because she had a strong feeling that she wasn't going to like what she was about to discover. Instead, she sucked it up and headed toward the truck, stopping a few feet away from Troy and his baby. If he had something to say, he could say it, and if not, she wasn't going to dig. She'd simply go to her house and pretend nothing had changed, even though her gut said that it had.

Troy did have something to say.

"I got news." He ran a hand over Livia's back. She twisted in his arms toward Kat, who was too far away to lean over and reach. "The guy I'm replacing at L&S isn't going to retire."

"There are probably other people in the area hiring," Kat said. "And you know that rent isn't a problem."

"I called my friend, Saskia, on the drive

back here, and I'm going to work for her on the Unrideable Tour."

"You're leaving?" The words were hard to push out, but she managed.

What about not wanting to raise your daughter on the road?

"One tour."

"Then you'll be back?"

He shook his head. "I don't think so," he said quietly.

"Why?" Kat no longer cared about digging.

"Because…" Livia started to cry, and Troy automatically rocked her against him, his gaze still fixed on Kat's face. "I need to take care of her."

Livia's whimpering quieted as soon as he spoke. Kat wished she could take it as a sign. "When do you leave?"

"Sass said she needed me yesterday. They lost a rider, and she's been using substitutes, but now that I'm signing on as part of the tour, printing programs will be easier."

She didn't smile at his attempt to lighten the mood. "I didn't expect you to leave so soon." There was a rawness to her words that surprised her.

"I have to."

"Maybe what I meant was that I didn't expect you to leave me." She spoke the truth and then swallowed. Her mouth was suddenly dry. She had not expected to speak the naked truth so easily. She'd barely been ready to acknowledge it herself, but there it was, hanging out there.

Troy started to speak and then apparently thought better of it. He looked past her as if gathering his thoughts. Or forming an argument.

"I know that I said all that stuff about healing from Derek and not trusting myself. I totally meant it. And I meant it when I said I wanted to be friends, and that was all. I meant it because I was afraid. But... I think I always thought we'd have time to see if things might change."

And now they didn't.

Not because he wasn't going to be on the farm but because she could see that he'd made up his mind not to risk letting something grow between them—not to acknowledge that it already had.

He was afraid of history repeating itself. She had the same fear, but not to the degree he did.

"Kat, I appreciate all you've done. It's been incredible being here."

"But…"

"I don't need to be rescued. I need to stand alone."

"Rescued?" Kat blinked at him and then closed her mouth after she realized it had fallen open. "You think I'm rescuing you? Do you think those were 'rescuing' kisses we shared?"

"I think there's an overlap."

For a moment, all she could do was to stare at him. Maybe she had felt those rescuing tendencies early on, as she had with her brothers, but…

She narrowed her eyes as a sudden thought struck her. "Do you *really* believe that, or are you saying it to make it easier to leave?"

"I have to leave, Kat."

He did. She could see it in the stiff way

he held himself, as if he were afraid of losing control. She glanced down at the ground and pulled in a breath as conflicting thoughts tangled in her brain. She wanted him to stay, but he needed to go.

Maybe it was because of his feelings for her coupled with his Kansas-sized pride. None of it was doing neither of them any favors.

She looked up. "If you have to leave, then go. But know this… I never saw myself as rescuing you. If you honestly believe that, it's your take. Don't try to make it mine."

"I know what I see. It's admirable that you put yourself out there for people."

"Admirable." The word fell like a stone.

"I care for you, Kat. But I can't—"

"Nor do you have to." She took a backward step, lifting her hands as if in surrender.

Livia, as if sensing something was off, pushed the top of her head against the side of his neck. "I don't want to leave things like this," he said.

"No, Troy. That's fine. You should leave things exactly like this." She gave a casual shrug. "It makes things easier in the long run." She looked over her shoulder at her house. "I may not see you before you go…"

She would not tell him to have a good life or that this wasn't over, though both thoughts shot through her head.

Troy hefted Livia higher in his arms, and it occurred to Kat that he was both protecting his child and using her as protection. She was his family, and he was afraid to expand. Afraid of loss. How was she supposed to battle that when she was just starting to understand her own fears and needs?

"I won't have time to help take the camp trailer back to your parents' ranch."

"That's fine. I'm going to rent it out. My brothers think I should have someone here on the farm. I'll have to start looking for my next rescue."

Those were not the words she wanted to use in place of goodbye, but that's what came out.

"I hope we can talk at a later date."

"And I hope you find what you're searching for, Troy. It's been good getting to know you."

With that, Kat Farley turned and walked out of Troy Mackay's life.

CHAPTER THIRTEEN

TROY'S HEART BEAT harder as his thumb hovered over his phone's keypad.

This is stupid. It's a call to your father.

Who might get in some emotional jabs or refuse to answer, but that was a risk Troy had to take. A risk Sass told him not to take after welcoming him aboard the Unrideable Tour, but he had to make certain his bases were covered if something happened to him. Or at least try. His profession was about to become exponentially more dangerous than it had been driving a gravel truck. His rodeo injuries, even the one that had temporarily ended his career, hadn't been life-threatening, but there was always that chance.

After packing his stuff the previous evening, he'd cleaned the trailer and called Walt to tell him what had happened. The old guy had grown on him, and he didn't want to leave without a word. He slept fitfully until dawn, and now he was making a call that he never would have made had it not been for Livia.

He pushed the button and turned the phone onto speaker so he could talk as he drove away from Littlegate Farm. His dad surprised him by picking up on the second ring.

He wasn't ready.

"Hello."

Silence followed his greeting, and Troy wondered if his dad was having trouble placing the voice. It had been almost five years since they'd spoken.

"Troy," his dad finally said.

The ball was in his court, but now that he had his dad on the line, all the scripts he'd practiced in his head evaporated. Words literally failed him.

"Is something wrong? Is your daughter all right?"

"Livia, your granddaughter, is fine. But she is the reason I'm calling."

"I'm listening."

"I need… I need to know that if something happens to me, Livia will be taken care of."

"Your mother and I are in no position to raise a child."

The flare of anger evoked by his father's words made it difficult for Troy to keep his tongue under control. There were so many things he could have said. Things not in Livia's best interest.

And why be angered by honesty?

Because they could have tried harder. He couldn't think of anything he wouldn't do for Livia.

He pulled in a breath, willed himself to stay calm.

"I'm thinking more in the financial sense." Nothing personal. Once upon a time he'd wanted more from his parents in that regard, but he had finally realized that no matter how many cliffs he jumped off, he wasn't going to get it. "This isn't an easy ask, Dad, but she is your granddaughter."

"What are you thinking?"

"Pretty much that you provide financial support for Livia if anything happens to me. I already have a guardian lined up, but any life insurance I'm able to get will not be enough to raise a child."

"Perhaps if you'd finished college."

Troy bit his tongue…for Livia's sake. "Perhaps," he agreed, though it cost him. "Dad, I made mistakes. Some of them on purpose."

"What do you mean?"

"When I was a kid. Trying to get your attention."

"You had my attention." His dad seemed genuinely mystified, and Troy sensed paternal hackles rising. His dad didn't like to be mystified.

"I made mistakes," he repeated. "I don't want the end result revisited on my kid. I'm only asking you to step in if something happens to me. I'm not asking for anything right now. Maybe not ever."

Another long silence, then his father said, "I'll speak to my lawyer in the morning. I can reach you at this number?"

The same number he'd had for a decade?

"Yes. I'll text you my email, too."

"I want to pick the guardian."

Troy's grip tightened on the phone. "Excuse me?"

"If I provide financial support, I want to make certain the child is raised according to my wishes."

"No." Troy would not set his daughter up for that. Better that Sass raise her on a shoestring budget, which she'd already volunteered to do when she tried to talk Troy out of contacting his dad.

"That's my stipulation."

"How are you going to find someone to raise a child? How are you even qualified to vet someone for that purpose?"

"Is that a commentary on your upbringing?"

"My upbringing was lonely."

"Your mother couldn't have more children."

"But maybe she—both of you—could have been parents."

A heavy silence followed the words, and Troy knew that he could kiss his kid's financial future goodbye. But the raw pain he'd felt since Livia's birth, when he'd discovered the strength of the parental bond, had broken through.

He was debating between attempting damage control and bowing to the inevitable when his dad said, "We gave you the freedom to explore. Heaven knows, we footed enough bills for extreme activities. Gave you carte blanche."

"You did." And his dad was never going to understand that Troy had been looking for structure. Parental support. Even if he could hammer the point home, what did he want from them now? An apology? An acknowledgment that they could have done better?

It wouldn't change anything, and it wouldn't soothe the bitterness he'd lived with for so long. That he was going to have to let go of on his own.

"I know I disappointed you by not following the path you set." College. Business degree, followed by law school.

"I gave up on that when you were fifteen. You were headstrong. Knew exactly what you wanted."

"Did you really believe that?"

It took his father a moment to say, "Of course."

"Huh."

"Huh?"

Holy smokes, his dad sounded almost human.

"I *was* headstrong," Troy admitted, wondering if his father would revert to his usual self the next time he spoke. "I had no idea what I wanted to do."

"We couldn't have known that being on the outside looking in."

Troy realized that his heart was beating faster. This was the closest thing he'd had to an in-depth conversation with his father in...forever? Yes. That was the time frame. "I was a rebellious kid." No sense getting into the hows and whys and segueing into the blame game. "It's possible that Livia will be the same. She's showing signs." He smiled a little. "But she's my kid. Your grandkid. I need to know she's provided for."

"Are you about to do something?"

"Just a job."

"Doing...?"

"Riding unrideable broncs," he said quietly.

"Troy." It sounded like his name had escaped his dad's lips before he could stop it from coming out. "Are you sure about this?"

"Why?"

"You're not exactly a spring chicken."

Troy couldn't keep from laughing. It was perhaps the last thing he'd expected to hear his father say.

"One tour will put me in good shape. I've had a few setbacks over the past year, but… like I said, one tour and I should be okay."

"Unless you get hurt or killed."

"There's that. And that's why I'm calling. For Livia."

"What if…what if I financed college for you?"

Troy felt his defenses rise, but he told himself that maybe throwing money at a problem was the only way his dad could deal emotionally. It wasn't like he didn't have his own issues engaging.

"If you want to finance college," he said gently, "start a fund for Livia, Dad." He held the phone a little tighter. "I got myself into this, and I'll get myself out."

"Who's the guardian you've chosen?"

"My boss on the tour. Saskia Belmont. She's a good person." Plus, she knew the value of laughter and a well-timed hug.

As did Kat.

But he wasn't allowing his thoughts to dwell there.

"She's honest, Dad. She wouldn't misuse Livia's money. I trust her."

"I'll talk to my lawyer."

"Thanks." Troy was torn between hanging up before his father could rescind the offer and wanting this unprecedented conversation to continue. He was talking to his dad. Like a person.

"How's Mom?"

"She and her friends are planning their annual getaway. Fiji, I think." The cool tone returned.

"Ah." Troy didn't know what else to say. "Well, like I said, you can reach me here, and I'll text my email." He swallowed. "I appreciate this, Dad."

"Yes." His father cleared his throat. "I'll be in touch."

"Right." Troy was about to end the call

when his father cleared his throat a second time.

"If…"

"Yeah?"

"If you wanted to send photos of Livia along with the email address, I'll share them with your mother."

"I'll do that." A bubble of something rose in his chest. Hope? He was never going to have the parents he'd needed, but maybe Livia would have grandparents.

He shot a glance at his sleeping daughter, knowing in his heart that no matter what she cooked up rebellionwise, he'd be there for her. She'd have a safe place in him. And if something happened to him, she would be provided for.

Troy was still debating about whether he and his dad might have hit a point where they could work out some kind of relationship when he drove into Larkspur. He fueled up his truck, much to Livia's displeasure, then returned the borrowed car seat to Daisy Lane, where he explained that Livia wouldn't need the full-time slot come September.

"I'm sorry to hear that," Daisy said, smiling as she touched Livia's arm.

Livia grinned back, which made Troy sorry, too. He'd found a place he trusted with his kid, and now he was moving on.

His last stop was on Main Street, where he was able to find parking less than a block from Dane Cashman's office. He got Livia out of her seat, told her they had mission, and then they'd be on their way to see Aunt Sass in Rock Springs, Wyoming.

Dane was alone in the front office. He was bent over the associate's desk and checking something on her computer when Troy carried Livia into the office.

"Glad I caught you," he said to Dane, who straightened as Troy approached.

"Are you looking for a place to buy or rent? I have a nice fixer-upper close to town that would be the perfect place to raise a family." He fixed Livia with his smarmy smile, but she refused to be impressed.

"Actually, I just stopped by to give you a bit of advice."

Dane made a show of being surprised, before making an *I'm game* face. "Shoot."

Troy crossed the room and came to a stop on the opposite side of the desk, enjoying the way that Dane's chin rose so he could meet Troy's eyes.

"If—" he put heavy emphasis on the word "—you cause *any* trouble for Kat Farley, I will hunt you down and do you bodily harm."

"Trouble?"

"Destroyed fences, stolen property. A fire."

The way Dane's expression changed at the mention of the fire convinced Troy that it had indeed been an accident. But the other stuff…yes. Dane had had a hand in it, and Troy wanted to make certain he didn't try any new tricks.

"I don't know what you're talking about."

"Think hard, because I'm dead serious about hunting you down if there are any repeat performances."

"Is that a threat?"

Could it possibly be interpreted as anything else?

Troy smiled. "Why don't we classify it as a promise?"

"I don't—"

"You do. And I'm here to tell you that I'm not putting up with it. Leave. Her. Alone."

"Or?"

Troy could see that Dane's bravado was more powerful than his sense of caution, which was a problem.

"Troublemaking can go two ways."

Dane gave him a disbelieving look.

"Even heard of Mackay Communications?" He caught the flicker of recognition in Dane's eyes. "I'm one of those Mackays. I *can* cause you harm, and I will. Leave Kat alone."

They stared at one another for a long, long moment, then Troy gave a dismissive nod.

"I'll be keeping tabs." And with that, Troy turned and left Dane Cashman's office, hoping that his bluff would buy Kat some peace. He was one of "those Mackays," but he had no clout in that regard. Total bluff. But the part about hunting the man down and doing him bodily harm—that Troy had been dead serious about.

He might not have anything to offer Kat.

He might not be ready to complicate his life by trying to raise an infant and start a relationship with a woman who deserved more than he was in a position to give, but he could watch her back.

CHAPTER FOURTEEN

KAT SWIPED HER paintbrush around the interior of the nearly empty paint can, loading the brush with just enough pale yellow paint to cover the last bare spot on the picket fence surrounding the front yard. She dropped the brush in the can and stood, flexing her back.

The fence looked good, as did the two smaller outbuildings she'd painted that week. She headed to the house to wash the brush, skirting the pots of asters she'd just bought to decorate the porch. One of the barn cats zipped past her, shooting under the porch. The little gray tabby, whom she'd named Sheila, was getting friendly, and if the cat wasn't careful, she'd end up being a house pet. Kat could use the company.

The work she was doing on the farm upped the charm factor, bringing it closer to what it had been when she'd visited her

Aunt Margo as a teen, but it wasn't helping with the empty feeling that had pervaded the place since Troy and Livia left. The camp trailer stood empty next to the barn, a constant reminder of the guy who was no longer in her life.

The guy who'd appeared out of nowhere, stolen her heart and then returned to the life he'd come from. She knew that he cared for her, but that knee-jerk fear of being abandoned, or coming to depend on something that could disappear from his life had proven to be too strong. They hadn't spent a lot of time together, but Kat knew that her life, her outlook, was forever changed because of Troy, just as it had been changed by discovering that Derek was playing her.

But the change with Troy had been positive. She'd loved working with him, hanging out with him, seeing him laugh. He'd been so closed off when they'd first met, but by the end of their time together, she'd known how to make him smile.

She missed Livia. The little girl had to be crawling by now. Three long weeks had passed since Troy had left, and Kat was certain the baby had hit other milestones.

She tapped the wet brush on the edge of the sink, laid it to dry on a folded towel and then headed to her freshly painted office to finish some spreadsheets. She'd just opened the file when her phone rang. She didn't know the number, but it was local, so she answered.

"This is Walt Stenson."

"Hi, Walt. Are you looking for Troy?"

"No. I have some information for you."

Kat brushed the curls back from her forehead. "I don't understand."

"Troy told me about the...interest in your farm, and I looked into it."

Walt Stenson looked into things? He was close to the bottom of the list of people Kat would have enlisted for stealth operations. Something about the grumpy factor.

"Not prying, mind you. Troy was concerned, and I have kind of a connection."

Kat took a seat. "I'd love to hear what you discovered."

"A group of investors are interested in buying the Bealman property, but they'll only make the deal if Margo's—your—farm is included. They're worried about access and the zoning is wrong. They're looking to make some kind of a spa hotel or something there, and if there are no neighbors, there's no one to protest the rezone from residential agricultural to business, or whatever they call it."

Kat took a moment to digest the information. "They kept it quiet." Which was impressive in a town the size of Larkspur.

"Rich folk can do that."

"Is Dane Cashman a potential investor, or is he just handling the sale for the Bealmans?"

"I did not ask."

Kat hesitated, before voicing the obvious question. "Who didn't you ask?"

"Gwen Bealman."

"Really?" Kat knew the name, but she had never met the woman. She was older than Kat's parents and had left the property with a caretaker when Kat was quite small.

"Yeah." Walt sounded oddly self-conscious. "I tracked her down via the class reunion website. She lives in North Carolina now, but we graduated high school to-gether. Class of sixty-six." He cleared his throat. "We also went to the senior prom."

"Did you wear a white sport coat?"

"No, but I had the pink carnation."

"I bet you were quite dapper."

Walt made a disparaging noise as Kat glanced out the window in the direction of the Bealman property. Thanks to Walt and Troy, she knew what she was up against.

Gwen Bealman living in North Carolina explained why the locals weren't abuzz. There was a good chance that Dane was the only one in the area who knew what was going on. And if his mouth was this tightly closed, then he was probably an investor. For all she knew, Derek was another.

"Thanks for the information, Walt." Kat pushed her curls back with one hand. "I think I'm going to have a chat with my local real estate agent."

"And maybe spread the word about the secret deal?"

"That's what I'm thinking."

"Have you heard from Troy?" Walt asked,

bringing Kat's plans for retribution to a skittering stop.

"I don't expect to." Which kind of ruined her. She missed the man and didn't know that there was anything she could do about it.

"I'm sorry to hear that."

There was a note in his voice that caused Kat to ask, "Because of your stud?"

"There's that, but because of him, too." Kat didn't say anything, sensing that if she stayed silent, Walt might have more to say. Her instincts proved correct. "He's…" Walt paused. "He's looking for something, but he won't let himself find it."

"You're right," she said softly. A perfect summary of Troy Mackay.

"I know."

Kat waited, hoping for more insight, but Walt had said his piece. "Thank you for the information, Walt. It helps to know what you're fighting against."

"Stick to your guns," he said.

"Thanks, Walt. Take care."

"Call if you need help."

"I will."

It was so odd. Most people gave Walt Stenson a wide berth, but maybe that was because he took such pains not to let anyone get too close. Did he have reasons for pushing people away?

Did she know anyone else with those qualities?

She stood with the phone in her hand, staring at the wall she intended to paint a cheery yellow in the next few days.

Walt had hit the nail on the head. Troy was searching for something he wouldn't allow himself to have. Why? If she called him on it, would it make a difference? Or would he stubbornly go his own way, convinced that he'd never have a family beyond his little girl?

Kat dropped her head back.

Of course.

Troy wanted a family, but he didn't know a family wanted him.

THE INAUGURAL UNRIDEABLE TOUR had put together top-ranked broncs—both saddle and bareback—bulls and high-scoring riders. They were four stops into the twenty-city tour, and it was already a raging success. Some cowboys came in as guest stars, but Troy would stay for the entire tour, earning points and trying to win a bonus prize at the end.

He hadn't ridden in almost a year, and although he'd continued his strength exercises, he hurt after night one. Then came night two, and he really hurt. But he'd ridden to the buzzer on the first night and had given it a good shot the second, getting thrown less than a second before his time was up. Even though there was a bonus for a successful ride, unlike the rodeo circuit, Troy got a salary just for showing up and getting on a bronc. It was like a regular job—except that his work partner wanted to stomp him into the ground.

Sass was getting into her duties as auntie, and while Troy could see that she found Livia adorable, she didn't have the same touch as Kat. When Livia had had one of her long crying jags, which Kat took in stride, Sass had been flummoxed. Calming the crying baby had become a challenge to be met. She'd stated that no one under the height of two feet four inches was going to get the better of her. Troy foresaw a tour-long battle of wills between his best friend and his baby.

Things would get easier when Livia got older, and he probably wouldn't be on the next tour, so it wouldn't be an issue. His body wasn't taking a beating the way it once had. This gig would set him up for the next phase of his life, which he was beginning to think might be college. He loved farrier work, but he needed something less seasonal, and frankly, he liked the idea of exploring a new horizon—maybe one that didn't take such a toll on his body.

He hadn't heard back from his dad, but that didn't worry him. Daniel Mackay was meticulous in his business dealings, and if he said he'd contact his lawyer about providing for Livia, he would. Troy just hoped he hurried, because the sooner he had Livia's future nailed down, the better.

He'd just heated a bottle on the tiny burner in the RV he'd rented for him and Livia to travel in when the phone rang. Certain that it was finally his dad calling to tell him what he'd decided about Livia, he answered without looking at the screen. He was surprised to hear Walt Stenson's rusty voice.

"Walt. Is everything all right? Is Jack okay?"

"He is. I wanted to let you know I talked to Kat Farley. Told her what I found out about her place."

"What did you find out?"

Walt explained that a group of investors were secretly looking at the property next door and wanted Kat's property as part of the deal.

"I hope she contacts her brothers about this," Troy said.

Walt gave him a look. "You don't think she can handle matters alone?"

"Yeah, I do." Kat was tough. Life on the Farley Ranch had prepared her for almost anything.

"But she shouldn't have to, right?"

"Right," Troy agreed on a cautious note.

"Then why should you?"

"Walt—"

"That's all I'm saying. Oh, and Kat plans

to meet up with that real estate guy. Give him a piece of her mind, I gather."

"When?"

"I have no idea. Maybe you could ask her."

TROY DID NOT ASK. Instead, he told Sass that after that night's performance, he'd be taking off and would rejoin the tour at their next stop in Lewiston, Idaho.

"Do you want me to babysit Button?" Sass asked.

"I'll take her." He and Livia were a team.

"I, for one, am not going to argue."

"You're relieved, aren't you?"

Sass grinned at him. "I'll stop by to get her before the grand entry. Unless you need her by the chutes to give you advice on Daffodil."

"I'm good. You two can cheer me on from the stands."

After the ride, Troy would collect his kid, and Sass could continue with the business of making certain the program ran smoothly. Once the performance was over, he and Livia were going to engage in something he liked to call driving all night. Or a good part of the night anyway.

And what was going to happen when he got home?

Not home. Littlegate Farm.

Once there, he'd explain to Kat that he'd already effectively threatened Dane, and if she wanted, they could do it again together. Let the guy know that if he messed with her, he was messing with a lot of other people, too.

And then…

He closed his eyes as he tried to picture "and then." He knew what he wanted. And he knew what he feared. They were practically the same thing.

He didn't know what to do about that.

An hour later, he was walking through fire as he was introduced to the crowd at the Missoula Civic Center. If he rode Daffodil tonight, he'd get the extra bonus, and since he was the only cowboy who'd ever ridden the mare, he was the last contestant before the bulls.

He did what he usually did before an event. He paced in the area behind the chutes, going over the ride in his head, using the adrenaline buzz to keep him focused. The stock was having a good night. So far, there'd been two successful rides and a lot of close calls. The crowd was eating it up.

When it was his turn on deck, he mounted the railings and straddled the black mare named for a bright yellow flower. Go figure. Once settled, he pounded his hand into rosined rope, checked his position by drawing his knees up and back.

He'd trained himself a long time ago not to listen to the announcer's hype, but tonight, he caught bits and pieces.

"…only cowboy to successfully ride this wily mare…" came through.

Right. He'd done it once; he'd do it again. This was what he was being paid for.

He drew in a long steadying breath and then nodded. The gate swung open. Instead of the pregnant pause that Daffodil was famous for, she followed the gate, exploding into the air.

Troy hadn't expected instant action, but he adjusted, muscle memory kicking in as he countered first the spinning bucks to the left, then some serious twists to the right.

Seven…six…five…

Daffodil was breathing heavily, possibly wondering what it was going to take to get this cowboy off her back. She dialed things up, jerking Troy sideways.

Four…three…two…

The black mare reared and pushed off with her back feet, buying air and doing a sunfish twist, attempting to show her belly to the lights above. She landed with a hellacious jolt to Troy's body as the buzzer blared and the crowd cheered.

The pickup man was in position, but before he could yank the strap around the mare's ticklish flank, she gave one last mighty buck, and Troy came off. He flipped over his hand, which was hung up in the rigging.

Troy fought to free his hand as he flopped at the horse's side. Another pickup man came in from the near side of the horse, leaning in to try to free Troy's hand.

By the time he slipped free of the rigging and landed in a heap on the ground, the crowd had gone quiet. The lizard part of his brain went into action, and he got to his feet, his body seeming to move of its own accord, because his brain wasn't having a lot of success telling his muscles what to do.

Dazedly, he headed toward the exit gate, vaguely aware of lifting his hat to the crowd and the answering cheers.

He was okay. He knew that, but he'd taken a beating, and he wasn't as young as he used to be.

But hey, he'd gotten the bonus. Money in the bank. *Cha-ching.*

"You okay?" the Justin Medical Team member asked as he exited the arena.

"Yeah." He just needed to get his daughter, get some ice and kick back for a while as he contemplated how to adjust his drive-all-night plan.

"Is this a typical day's work?"

Troy stopped in his tracks, wondering if he'd hit his head harder than he thought when he'd finally broken free. "Dad?"

"I was in the area."

"Were you?"

"New offices in Missoula."

"I didn't realize you had anything that wasn't on the coast."

His father shrugged. "We're moving into Montana and Wyoming. Since I was here, I wanted to watch you do what you do." He gave Troy a look that clearly said he didn't understand his son's chosen career.

"Not every night is this spectacular," Troy said as he started toward the exit. "But it's a rough sport. This is my last season."

"Then what?"

"I don't know. But I'll figure something out." He gave his father an uncertain smile. "It's kind of what I do now." Figure things out as the powers that be flung obstacles at him.

His dad didn't reply. "I also thought I might meet my granddaughter. Which I did."

"How?"

"I asked about you and was directed to a woman with an odd name."

Troy's head was clearing. Nothing like the shock of seeing a long-lost parent to cause your brain to shift gears. "Saskia?"

"She had Livia and introduced me, but she wouldn't let me hold her."

Troy smiled a little. They stopped just outside the exit, and Daniel Mackay put his hand on Troy's shoulder. Troy, in turn, barely suppressed a wince.

"I have the wheels rolling on the trust for Livia," his father said. "That said…maybe you could find a profession that allows you to sit at a desk."

"I can't think of anything worse," he said honestly. "But there are a few other things I might want to try my hand at."

Daniel glanced at his watch, a habitual movement that Troy had forgotten until now.

"I have a jet waiting at the airport."

"Of course."

"I'd like to get together again." He straightened his shoulders. "I'd like to get to know my granddaughter."

"I'm glad." If he was expecting his father to say something along the lines of how he was ready to be a parent, it didn't happen. But there was something different about his father. Almost a humility that hadn't been there before. Perhaps life had taught him a few lessons, too.

"I'll be in touch. I mean it."

Troy nodded. "Thanks for coming, Dad."

His dad smiled and held out a hand, lightly grasping Troy's upper arm as they shook. And again, Troy managed not to wince. The mare had done a number on him.

He watched as his dad walked away, hands deep in the pockets of his expensive overcoat. They'd never have a traditional relationship, but maybe they could have something. And maybe Livia would have grandparents. Or a grandparent. He still didn't know where his mother stood on all of this.

One obstacle at a time.

He drew in a breath as his dad disappeared and then headed toward the RV to grab a quick shower before collecting Livia from Sass. He ran a hand over the shoulder that Daffodil had nearly dislocated and stopped as he caught sight of a car that looked familiar.

He cocked his head as he approached.

A gray Camry with a brand-new windshield was parked next to his RV. And as he stood stupidly gawking at it, the door opened, and Kat Farley stepped out.

CHAPTER FIFTEEN

A BRUISE WAS starting to bloom on Troy's cheek, puffing up the skin beneath his eye. Arena dirt clung to his shirt and chaps, and there was a smear across his jaw, which he brushed at with the back of his hand as he walked toward her.

Kat had never in her life seen a more perfect man. And she didn't know what she was going to do about it.

She stayed close to her car as Troy approached, and when he came to a stop a few feet in front of her... words failed her.

Kat had practiced what she wanted to say as she'd driven—long speeches, short speeches. Pithy speeches, tender speeches. Not a word came to her.

It was Troy who broke the silence.

"Kat?" Her name was both a statement and a question.

She lifted her chin, ready to wing it. For better or worse, they were doing this.

"I wanted to talk to you before you left the state," she said. After Missoula, the tour headed into Idaho and then Washington, Oregon, California.

Troy nodded and to her dismay, she couldn't read him. Couldn't tell if he was glad to see her, or if she'd come at the worst possible time. Her stomach, which had started tightening as soon as she caught sight of him walking with an older man toward the RV, was now a bona fide walnut.

"Did you see my ride?"

She shook her head. "I got here too late."

He gestured to the RV with his head. "How'd you know which one was mine?"

"A quick question at the gate." She smiled a little. "You might warn them about stalker fans." But she was glad that the contestant gatekeeper had so easily let loose with the information.

"Noted." He shifted his weight as he hooked a thumb into the belt of his batwing chaps.

For a long moment they studied one another, silent tension building until something seemed to break inside of Troy. The mask lifted, and his expression shifted, taking on a look of longing and…pain…and…uncertainty.

"I was coming to see you." His voice was low and rough-edged.

Kat's lips parted. "You were?"

"I figured I could rejoin the tour in Idaho."

He glanced past her toward his RV, making her wonder if Livia was in there with a sitter, but when he looked back at her, she knew that his daughter was not at the center of his thoughts.

"There are things I need to say." He held her gaze as if daring her to look away.

"I have things, too. That's why James is watching Littlegate Farm."

Troy frowned. "You left James in charge of your farm?"

"I did, but it'll be okay because I banned fire and scissors."

The next thing she knew, she was in Troy's arms, drawing in the scent of dust, horse, leather and man.

She'd foreseen a lot of talking, convincing, head-beating on the bit of granite that was Troy Mackay. Instead, she was being held tightly against the long hard body of the man she loved.

"Are you trying to tell me something," she murmured against the dusty cotton of his official Unrideable Tour shirt.

"I need you. I haven't stopped thinking about you."

Kat went still and then tightened her grip on his back, pressing herself against him.

"I need you, too," she said. "So much."

She didn't know how long they held each other in the parking lot next to her car. She only knew she didn't want to let go of him.

"It's scary, isn't it?"

She smiled against his shirt and tilted her head up to look into his blue eyes. "Terrifying. Maybe that's a good thing."

"If you say so." She felt him swallow before he said, "I don't have a good track record as far as relationships go. Any relationship, except for maybe with Sass."

"Do you know what family is about, Troy?"

"I can't say I've had a ton of experience there."

"Family is about having one another's back, like you had mine with Dane. Family is about working side by side through adversity and celebrating side by side during the good times" She brought her hands up to frame his face. "It's not about being perfect and having a life that's challenge-free. Because a partner, a real partner, will help you through everything."

Troy eased her against him, holding her loosely, and she felt his chest rise and fall. "I'd not ask anyone to share in my troubles," he said.

"But someone might volunteer." She lightly touched his face where a frown had formed. "I volunteer, and it's *not* a rescue."

"You want to make a family?"

"I want to keep it open as an option. I know you have stuff you want to take care of first, but I'm telling you that we can take care of it together." She smiled a little. "I'm patient, and I'm flexible, Troy. I can wait until the end of the tour. I can move. But I want a chance."

"So do I." He touched his forehead to hers. "I want to do battle with that twerp Cashman, and I want to get hay fields in order, and I want to spend the evenings with you and Livia."

"We can do that, you know."

"We can probably do anything we want."

"I think so," she agreed.

"My dad was just here."

Kat gave him a stunned look. "For real. Was that him walking with you?"

"Yeah. He wants to get to know Livia."

"How do you feel about that?"

"He wasn't the perfect parent. But I've let that color my life for too long. I'm open to new beginnings." He reached down to take her hand and threaded his fingers through hers. "On many fronts."

"I like this front," she said, squeezing his fingers before rising up on her toes to kiss him. "You're dusty."

"I'll shower," he said. "And when I'm done, we'll get Livia and grab a bite."

"Kind of like a family?"

He smiled down at her and twisted a curl around his finger. "Exactly like a family."

"By the way, James has a line on Arlie. He might be able to get your money back."

Troy smiled. "That would be great. But you know what…maybe we can just let him keep it. I think he might have accidentally done me the biggest favor of my life."

Kat squeezed his hand again. "I think you might be right."

EPILOGUE

"THAT'S ONE BEAUTIFUL ANIMAL," Whitney said, leaning on the fence rails as she watched Kat's new charge, a flashy bay Standardbred mare, cross the pasture with long floating strides.

"She could use a little of you," Kat said, shifting to keep Livia's hands away from Whitney's hair.

"Meaning?"

"She's spoiled. Disrespectful to her owner, who's just a teensy bit afraid of her."

"Ah." Whitney settled her chin on her hands. "Would that I could."

"Why can't you?" Maddie asked before looking past Whitney to where smoke was rolling out of one of the two barbecues that James and Troy were manning.

"It's fine," Kat said to Maddie. "James has a 'technique' for flavoring hamburgers. "It actually works."

"Okay," Maddie said dubiously. "I just wish Cody could have been here to help. He's great with a grill."

Cody, Maddie's fiancé, hadn't attended either of the last two get-togethers Kat and Maddie had arranged when Whitney came home for the weekend. He was also a "maybe" for the Friendsgiving celebration they were planning for the Saturday before Thanksgiving.

Kat was concerned, and judging from the way Whitney avoided answering their friend, she felt the same.

"He's so busy with his job," Maddie continued. "I'm looking forward to being married so we see more of one another." She gave Kat a look. "You know what I mean."

Kat did. Troy still had another two months of touring with the Unrideable before he was done with rodeo forever, but he made it back to Littlegate Farm whenever there was a long break in his schedule. Twice James had watched the farm so that Kat could join Troy on the road.

Livia leaned toward Maddie who took

the little girl into her arms before turning to Whitney.

"What is stopping you from taking on a few horse training jobs?"

"I think it has something to do with no facilities." Whitney had planned to train horses for a living until reality reared its ugly head and she realized that she wanted more job security than freelance horse training offered.

"But…" Kat said with an encouraging lift of her eyebrows "…if you moved home you could train on the side. Right?"

It was no secret that Whitney did not love her job. That she had become the office manager of a major insurance firm in Missoula for security, not satisfaction.

"I will. One day." She sounded wistful.

"Life is short," was all Kat said in return. Maddie nodded and then Livia launched herself toward Whitney, who laughed as she took the little girl.

"Making the rounds, are we?" Whit asked the baby before glancing at Kat. "She's going to be the cutest flower girl."

Kat went still. "Troy and I haven't—"

"Right," Whitney said.

"Will Arlie be the best man?" Maddie asked innocently. "He did bring you together."

A shout from the general direction of the barbecues had them turning in unison, then Kat pressed her hand to her mouth as she watched her brother fight fire with a spray bottle.

"Talk about smokey flavor," Maddie murmured.

"The burgers are already on a plate," Kat said as they started toward the cooking area. "See them on the table there?"

"Oh. Good." Whitney let out a whooshing breath. "I'm hungry."

By the time they reached the cooking area, the fire was out, and James was fanning the smoke away with a dish towel.

"In the nick of time," Troy said, looping an arm around Kat's shoulders. He leaned down to give her a light kiss as Whitney, still holding Livia, and Maddie started arranging things on the picnic table.

"What happened?" Kat nodded at the

still smoking barbecue. "Did James's secret method get away from him?"

"No. The hot pad fell onto the coals."

"Ah." Kat made a mental note as to what to get her brother for Christmas—a stack of barbecuing hot pads.

"I see the burgers are done," Andrew called as he came out of the house carrying a bowl of potato salad. Kent followed with a container of coleslaw.

Kat met Troy's gaze as her brothers headed to the picnic table and murmured, "They're onto us."

"What?" he asked in a low voice before shooting a look at the table. Whit gave him a small wave before he turned back to Kat. "No way."

"I know, but they're talking best men and flower girls."

"Huh."

Troy had proposed during a tour stop in Pendleton, Oregon, driving Kat to a spot along the Columbia River and literally dropping to one knee. She'd said yes, and then they'd agreed to keep their betrothal quiet until after Maddie's wedding at the end of December.

"Maybe you should embrace your inner Farley and tell everyone that we got engaged three months after our first kiss."

She smiled up at him. "Or maybe we'll wait until after Maddie's wedding."

It wasn't that she was afraid of stealing Maddie's thunder, but rather that she enjoyed holding this secret between them until they had definite plans.

"They know," Troy said as Maddie murmured something to Andrew who glanced furtively at Kat and Troy before nodding agreement. Troy turned back to Kat. "Maybe my dad told them."

Kat gave him a shocked look. "Your dad knows?"

"He wormed it out of me."

Kat rolled her eyes then turned to her family, her hand resting on Troy's arm.

"Listen up." When all five faces were turned her way, she said, "We're getting married. We don't have a date, but it won't be until after Livia is walking so that she can be flower girl."

A whoop went up from the table as Kat turned to her groom-to-be and smiled up into his amused face. Things had happened quickly between them, but they felt right. In fact, nothing in Kat's life had ever felt as right as sharing her life with this man and his daughter.

"There," she said. "Inner Farley embraced." She gave his chest a pat. "Shall we eat smokey burgers to celebrate?"

Troy leaned down to take her lips in a sweet kiss, prompting a chorus of groans and cheers from friends and family.

"Yes," he said simply. "Let's."

* * * * *

Be sure to look for the next book in The Cowgirls of Larkspur Valley series by Jeannie Watt, available wherever Harlequin Heartwarming books are sold!